*Jack Vance*

# Vandals of the Void

Jack Vance

# Vandals
# of the Void

Spatterlight
P R E S S
340 S. Lemon Ave #1916
Walnut, CA 91789

www.jackvance.com

# Foreword

TODAY IS A WONDERFUL TIME to be alive — the most exciting and colorful age in the whole tremendous history of man. We are in a period of change-over, from a civilization based on European ideas that has lost its momentum and grown tired, to a new civilization on whose basic patterns we are still working.

No one could call this an era of calm; quite the reverse. Events come at us with a rapidity that bewilders most people and alarms not a few. Of these, some take refuge in the past; they occupy their leisure with folk-dancing, historical novels; they collect antiques and live in 'period' houses. Others deny that the world is changing; these are the people who shrug off scientists and mathematicians as 'long-hairs' and 'absent-minded professors', and consider science fiction the sole province of escapists.

The naked fact is that we are changing from one way of life to another with a speed that is not only unparalleled: it is astonishing. Science fiction provides a primary education for this new age exactly as history and geography books have educated us for the present. Science fiction gives us a head start at fitting ourselves to the new conditions, and we have an enormous advantage over people who ignore the future.

Twenty years ago only scientists and readers of science fiction knew the meaning of the words 'atomic energy' and 'space travel'. Even today many people dismiss space travel as an idea in the same class with astrology and the Easter bunny. The truth is that space travel is almost as close as tomorrow. Plans and progress are military secrets at the moment, but guessing is not only free; it's fun. Here are my guesses.

By 1965 spaceships powered by chemical energy will land human beings on the moon.

By 1968 spaceships will cross to Mars and Venus, and assume satellite orbits above the upper limits of the Martian and Venusian atmospheres. A man will ride a small glider-rocket to the surface of each planet. After one, two, perhaps three days of exploration, he will strip off the glider wings, fly the rocket fuselage back to the mother ship.

By 1975 permanent satellite stations will circle Earth, Mars and Venus.

By 1978 atomic energy will be adapted to the propulsion of spaceships.

By 1980 permanent colonies such as the Security Station on the Moon, Miracle Valley on Venus, Perseverine on Mars will come into existence. The potential animal, vegetable, mineral resources of our neighboring worlds will be explored and undergo development. Freight costs will be very high; it will be economical to export to Earth only commodities of high intrinsic value, such as fur, musk, precious metals and woods, jewels, perfume and aromatic oils, jade, ivory, coral, native handiwork and fabrics (if any), fossils and zoological specimens, other objects beyond conjecture.

These shipments will inevitably tempt dishonest men too lazy to work for themselves, but who are willing to live as parasites on the effort and enterprise of other men.

By 1985 the age of space piracy will begin.

Just as a plant requires a hospitable environment of soil, sunlight, air and water in which to grow, so a flourishing state of piracy requires special conditions. These include reasonable security of operation, cargoes which represent concentrated wealth, a ready market for stolen goods.

In space, conditions will be favorable — at first. The asteroid belt beyond Mars, for instance, offers a refuge where a pirate ship might hide indefinitely without fear of radar detection. Cargoes will be rich and unprotected. For every dishonest man in space, twenty on Earth will help him dispose of his spoils.

Inevitably law and order will spread through space. A police force will be established, a Space Navy. Pirates will cease to be a threat, at least in the region around the Solar System.

## Foreword

The age of space pirates will probably occur during the lifetime of us all. Quite possibly some of you reading these words will enlist in the Space Navy. I hope that none of you serve with the pirates. If you do, I'm sure you'll regret it. The pay might not be so good in the Space Navy, but you'll live longer.

J.V.

# CONTENTS

Chapter I: Farewell to Venus . . . . . . . . . . . . . . . . . . . . . . . . 1

Chapter II: Graveyard of Space . . . . . . . . . . . . . . . . . . . . 10

Chapter III: Ghostly Ruins . . . . . . . . . . . . . . . . . . . . . . . . 19

Chapter IV: The Killer Eye . . . . . . . . . . . . . . . . . . . . . . . . 26

Chapter V: Pirate Fever . . . . . . . . . . . . . . . . . . . . . . . . . 36

Chapter VI: Moon Treasure . . . . . . . . . . . . . . . . . . . . . . 45

Chapter VII: The Perfect Crime . . . . . . . . . . . . . . . . . . . . 52

Chapter VIII: The Coded Message . . . . . . . . . . . . . . . . . 61

Chapter IX: Blood on the Moon . . . . . . . . . . . . . . . . . . . 70

Chapter X: The Thing with the Golden Eyes . . . . . . . . . . . . 79

Chapter XI: The Basilisk Stirs . . . . . . . . . . . . . . . . . . . . 87

Chapter XII: Human Satellite . . . . . . . . . . . . . . . . . . . . 93

Chapter XIII: The Basilisk Strikes . . . . . . . . . . . . . . . . . . 99

Chapter XIV: Crazy Sam's Notebook . . . . . . . . . . . . . . . 107

Chapter XV: Flood of Fire . . . . . . . . . . . . . . . . . . . . . . 115

Chapter XVI: The Eyes of the Basilisk (I) . . . . . . . . . . . . . . 121

Chapter XVII:  Lost in the Lunar Caves . . . . . . . . . . . . . . . .130

Chapter XVIII:  The Eyes of the Basilisk (II) . . . . . . . . . . . .137

Chapter XIX:  The Great Martian Raid . . . . . . . . . . . . . . . .142

Chapter XX:  Attack!. . . . . . . . . . . . . . . . . . . . . . . .148

Chapter XXI:  Battle . . . . . . . . . . . . . . . . . . . . . . . .154

Chapter XXII:  A Glimpse at the Future . . . . . . . . . . . . . . .159

# CHAPTER I

## *Farewell to Venus*

THE DEVIL'S CITADEL, a volcanic plug of massive black gabbro, rose a sudden, sheer and astonishing two thousand feet, dominating Miracle Valley like a stump in a garden patch. Jamatula River made a looping detour around the base, with the clean white town of Miracle Valley strung along its banks. The top surface was flat, as if the Citadel were indeed the petrified stump of an ancient and colossal world-tree.

From platform at the base to landing-stage at the top stretched a cable, frail as a spiderweb beside the bulk of the Citadel. A lift car rose up the cable; inside, by a window, stood Dick Murdock, traveling bag at his feet, binocular case and camera slung over his shoulder.

He looked with wistful intensity along the valley, where his home showed white in a glade of the green, red and blue forest. Already the landscape was blurring; hazy golden light flooded Miracle Valley like warm honey. It was hard to avoid a feeling of loss; homesickness had come upon him even before he was out of sight of home.

A voice said in his ear, "Traveling alone, young fellow?"

Dick turned, looked up into yellow eyes, intent and wide apart in a strange falcon-face. The skin was dusky-sallow; the hair was a peculiar mustard color, soft and thick as fur. The forehead was narrow; the nose cut down like a sickle, thin and close to the face, with a subtle hook to the tip. The mouth was pale, almost lipless, like a knife slit.

Dick said, with what dignity he could muster, "Yes, I'm traveling alone."

"Come out alone from Earth?"

Dick shook his head. "I was born on Venus."

"Oh!" The man's eyebrows rose, the rest of his face rigid as a mask. He glanced up toward the eternal overcast. "You'll be seeing sun and stars for the first time."

"The second time. Last year I flew up to the meteorological station with my father — fifty miles above the clouds."

The man made no comment, but stood as if listening.

Dick studied him covertly, his lobe of curiosity, never lethargic, aroused: what was he hearing? Dick heard nothing but the voices of the other occupants of the car.

"In that case," said the man absently, "your father must be connected with the Cosmic Ray Research Institute."

"He founded it," said Dick, "the same year I was born."

"Well, well." The man still seemed to be listening.

Dick strained his ears. A murmur of voices came to him. "...over-dramatic, too fanciful to be taken seriously."

"There's nothing fanciful about death."

"But what is a basilisk?"

"As I understand, it's a legendary monster; if you looked into its eyes you couldn't move."

"That's ridiculous!"

The voices dropped. Dick heard the words, "*Canopus* and *Capella*, in one month —" He remembered reading of the *Canopus* and *Capella* mystery, two ships lost on the Mars run; where was the connection with a basilisk?

A gust of wind caught the car, swung it out sharply. The mutter of conversation became gasps, exclamations. Dick reached for the rail, stumbled, clutched the coat of the man with the falcon-face.

The man jerked, clapped a hand to his pocket, fixed Dick with yellow eyes instantly suspicious.

Surprised at the violent reaction to his touch, Dick stammered, "I'm sorry, I didn't mean to..." The words died in his throat.

The man turned to the window. Dick, with a speculative glance at the pocket, moved a step away.

The truss at the top landing hung over them. The car shivered, stopped, thumped against the stage. A porter wrapped in a blue trench coat stepped out of a long low building. Leaning against the wind he crossed the platform, locked the gangplank to the ship, and slid back the car door. A gust rushed in smelling of rain and damp rock.

Gingerly the passengers crossed the gangplank, pushed through the wind to the concrete building.

Dick craned his neck for a view of the spaceship, peering between bodies, looking over shoulders, but caught only a tantalizing glimpse. He was last out of the car. Instead of running for the protection of the building, he stood swaying with the wind rushing past his ears, blowing tears into his eyes. Two hundred yards across the rock stood the *African Star*.

Dick had seen pictures of hypothetical spaceships, drawn by imaginative artists before the actuality of spaceflight. Invariably the depicted shapes were long and pointed, like darts. Perplexed by the contrast with the squat ships of reality, Dick had taken the matter up with his father. Dr. Murdock had glanced at one of the pictures in question. "Well, in the first place, Dick, there's a vast difference between an illustrator and an engineer. The illustrator paints a ship to look at, the engineer has the thankless job of building a ship to fly — a completely different matter. The imaginative artist, oddly enough, uses very little imagination; he models his spaceship after the pattern of airplanes, skyrockets, arrows, birds, fish — shapes which either by design or evolutionary development slide through air or water with the least resistance. The natural element of the spaceship is space." He inspected Dick quizzically. "What natural forms do we find in space?"

Dick, not quite sure what was expected of him, had answered, "Stars and planets are all spheres."

"Exactly. The engineer designs his ship to function in its natural medium, which is space, not air or water. Streamlining on a spaceship is like a buggy whip on an automobile, feathers on an airplane. The spaceship leaves the planet slowly, lands slowly. Air resistance counts for nothing. The important characteristics are lightness and rigidity. Even with atomic energy we try to be careful with weight; every pound put in useless structure is a pound less pay load. A sphere encloses the most volume for the least surface; however, the necessity for a stable landing base and bracing for the thrust-tubes induces the engineer to elongate the hull."

Considering the businesslike bulk of the *African Star*, Dick remembered his father's words. Certainly there was no faddish streamlining about the *African Star*; the shape perfectly expressed the purpose which it was designed to serve. He turned away, and driven by a great buffet of wind, ran across to the terminal depot. Inside, he fell into the line which slowly advanced past a check desk. Ahead of him was the man with the falcon-face.

The agent was a brisk little man with bottle-brush red eyebrows and bright blue eyes. One by one the passengers filed past him, the agent glancing into their hand luggage.

"Name, please?" He was speaking to the man ahead of Dick.

"A. B. Sende."

The agent ticked off a name on the passenger roster. "Berth 14, Mr. Sende." He glanced at Sende's briefcase. "Do you carry any seeds, insects, fungus, spawn, spores, eggs, any product or native habitant of Venus, alive or dead, on your person or in your baggage?"

"No."

"Very well. But in any event, I'll take a look into your briefcase."

Sende hesitated; Dick saw his fingers tighten around the handle. "There's nothing in it but private papers."

"Sorry, Mr. Sende. I've got to look."

Sende gave up his briefcase. The agent opened it, squinted inside, handed it back. "Can't risk importing new pests to Earth, Mr. Sende."

"No. Is that all?"

"That's all. You can go aboard or you can sit in the waiting room. We take off as soon as we hear from the *American Star*; she's a day overdue already."

"What's that?" Sende spoke in a sharp voice. "A day overdue?"

"That's what I said. A day overdue."

Sende turned on his heel and walked swiftly through the door.

The agent, craning his neck, looked after him. "Humph," he grunted. "Queerer and queerer every trip." His fierce blue eyes focused on Dick. "Yes boy? What's your name?"

Dick was taken a little aback. "Dick Murdock."

"Well, well." The agent glanced behind Dick. "All by yourself?"

"Yes."

"Nothing wrong with that. When I was your age —" he looked sharply at Dick from under his bristling red eyebrows "— about fourteen, I take it?"

"I was fifteen last week."

"Humph. A little on the slim side, I'd say. Need fattening up. Good hard work will do the trick. Well, when I was your age I had a little fishing sloop off the Great Barrier Reef, did a bit of pearl-diving when the tide was good, and the Control out of sight." He chuckled. "Well, that's long ago." He darted a swift glance at Dick. "Are you any relation to Dr. Paul Murdock?"

"He's my father."

"Now, think of that," said the agent softly, placing both hands on the desk. "Then you'll be joining your father on the moon?"

"Yes," said Dick. "He's been appointed Chief Astronomer at the Lunar Observatory. Next year my mother and sister will probably be coming out."

"Then you're leaving Venus for good."

"Well, I hope to come back sometime."

"You'll find it bleak out there, nothing like Miracle Valley." He bent over the roster, checked off Dick's name. "But then, maybe you'll like it. There's scenery like nothing imaginable — mountains going straight up till you give yourself a crick looking for the top. I was there in the bad old days, when the Security Station was going. Now a person doesn't hear much about the moon; it's out of fashion, with people coming and going to Mars and Venus and beyond and all the beautiful trinkets flooding back to Earth…Well, Dick, you're in Berth 22 with a nice porthole looking out on nothing." He eyed Dick's handbag. "And what kind of livestock might you be carrying?"

"None that I know of."

"Well, let's take a look. We can't afford to have any man-o-war bugs turned loose on Earth, pets or not." He opened Dick's bag; his eyebrows bristled up as if electrified. "My word, what's this? A bombsight?"

Dick laughed. "That's an electric binoculars. It's a little bulky, but by twisting this dial I get any power of magnification up to 200."

"Heavens above, and what'll they think of next? And this gadget, what's the nature of this? It looks like something straight from the booby hatch."

Dick said with dignity, "That's my portable radio. I built it myself. It works."

The agent looked doubtfully into the bag. "I can't put my hand down in there for fear of having something snap on it."

"There's nothing dangerous. I'll take it all out if you like."

The agent snapped the bag shut. "Don't bother. I'll give you a clean bill of health on your reputation. You can go aboard or you can wait."

Dick looked out the window to the silhouette of the ship. "I think I'll go aboard."

"Have a good trip, and my regards to your father."

"Thank you." Dick crossed the waiting room, slid back the door, pushed out upon the windy face of the Devil's Citadel. With his head bowed and gusts roaring past his ears, he walked up under the hull, climbed the loading ramp, stepped through the entrance port. A tall broad-shouldered Negro sat at a desk reading a thick book with a half-abstracted, half-angry frown. He wore a neat blue and gray uniform, a cap with 'Boatswain' in gold letters across the front.

He looked up, put down his book. "Name, please?"

"Dick Murdock."

The bosun glanced at his list, drew a line through Dick's name. "Your berth is No. 22, straight around the ladder to Stage 2."

"Thanks." Dick hesitated a moment. "How long before take-off?"

The bosun looked up into the sky, glanced at his watch. "As soon as the *American Star* lands we'll be off. She's twenty-six hours overdue."

"But why are we waiting for the *American Star*?"

"There's Earth mail aboard — if it arrives."

"*If* it arrives? Why shouldn't it arrive?"

The bosun grinned. "I didn't mean to be caught quite like that."

Dick persisted, "Has there been bad news about the *American Star*?"

"No news at all."

"Isn't that rather strange?"

"'Strange' is hardly the word for it. It's downright alarming, when you think that two ships disappeared from the Mars run last month."

"But why — how —"

"Perhaps they hit meteors. Perhaps..." He paused.

"Perhaps what?"

The bosun shrugged. "Strange things happen. It's nothing new if I tell you space is a strange place." He looked down toward the terminal building. "I'd do better keeping my mouth shut. If the captain heard me talking like this and scaring the passengers, he'd skin me head to foot."

"I won't say anything." Dick twisted to look at the bosun's book. "What are you reading?"

The bosun was obviously relieved at the change of subject. "Kant's *Critique of Pure Reason.* It's the finest book in the world for a space-man." He laughed at Dick's expression. "I never get finished with it, it's always just as if I'm flipping back the cover for the first time. And if I do get to the back page I can start all over, because I haven't understood it from the time before." He shook his head at the book in rueful admira-tion. "Even granted that I do get it licked in the normal way, it still isn't worn out, because I can always start at the back and read word for word backward to the front. That makes it two books in one, and it makes equal sense either way."

Dick was fascinated with the idea. "Don't you get bored with it?"

"Oh, no." The bosun slapped his big dark hand affectionately on the cover. "It's a game the three of us play — Kant, me and the book. I fig-ure the score to be something like the book, 20; Kant, 8; me, 2."

Dick laughed with great amusement. "I'm not very sporting. I'd only read books that let me win."

"It's a good idea once in a while," the bosun admitted, "just to keep up your morale. I've learned Sanskrit, Chinese, and Russian; I can play the zither, the oboe, the concertina and the mandolin; I know the phys-iology of birds and psychology of ants, the geography of Venus and the geology of Mars. But they all give up too quick, and a spaceman has a lot of time on his hands." He patted the book again. "Here's something a man can sink his teeth into, something that fights back."

"You should try mathematics," said Dick. "I've gone a few rounds myself with algebra and geometry."

The bosun considered. "Perhaps that's a good thought." He looked critically at the book. "I'll have to admit that I suspect old Mr. Kant of cheating. As soon as I think I've got him pinned down, he changes the meaning of a few words, and I'm left thumbing back to Chapter Three."

From the waiting room a horn roared flatly over the wind. The bosun rose to his feet. "There's the stand-by signal and here comes Captain Henshaw and the mate. Looks like we're not going to wait any longer."

Captain Henshaw marched up the ramp, a short, solid man with heavy white hair, a grim mouth and a nutcracker jaw. Behind him came the mate, a dark young man in an immaculate uniform. He wore a luxuriant handle-bar mustache, the like of which Dick had never before seen.

The captain nodded politely to Dick, turned to the bosun. "How's it look, Henry?"

"Everybody aboard, Cap'n. This lad here is the last."

"Seal up, then. What's the word from Merrihew?"

"Tubes all warm, ready for take-off."

"Good. Take-off as soon as we check instruments."

"Any news from the *American Star*, sir?"

"Not a peep. But we can't wait." Captain Henshaw turned to Dick. "I'll have to ask you to take to your berth for a few hours. We're leaving on two-gravity acceleration. Know what that means?"

"I think so," said Dick. "We'll be rising twice as fast as an object would fall to the ground."

"Right. You'll weigh twice as much as you do now, and you're much better off in your berth."

Dick nodded, flipped his hand to Henry and went on into the ship.

Cabin 22 was a cubicle about six feet on a side. The berth lay along the outside hull with a small square porthole over the pillow. Dick's two suitcases, plastered with red, blue and white spaceship *African Star* labels, occupied a rack to his right; at his left a magnesium washbasin folded into the wall, with a mirror above.

A speaker built into the wall clicked and hummed. A voice said, "Attention, personnel and passengers: take-off in five minutes. Passengers are requested to take to their bunks."

Dick slipped off his shoes, removed his jacket, stretched out. At a knock on the door he raised up. "Come in."

A pretty stewardess looked through the doorway. "Take-off in three minutes, please keep to your berth."

She closed the door. Dick heard her knock at the next cabin, heard her say, "Take-off in three minutes." He lay back, tense with excitement.

The wall-speaker hummed; the voice said, "Take-off in one minute."

Dick watched the seconds tick off on his watch: twenty — ten — five — three — two — one — the ship trembled, lurched, swept smoothly up. The berth sagged under Dick's weight; his body felt as if he were buried in sand, and for a moment he had trouble catching his breath.

A long minute went by. Clouds suddenly whitened the port, boiled past. A moment later they were gone. Sunlight poured hotly through the square port; the sky was pure ultramarine, swiftly darkening as the ship rose toward the limits of the atmosphere. Then the sky went black, the stars shone in glittering multitudes and Venus was left behind.

# CHAPTER II

## Graveyard of Space

TIME PASSED, PLEASANT, MONOTONOUS HOURS. Dick read microfilm books from the ship's library, watched the daily movie, listened to the news broadcast, tinkered with his portable radio. He wandered everywhere about the ship, from the navigation dome to the cargo holds loaded with purple amber from Great Banshee Swamp. He talked at great lengths with Henry the bosun, and even dipped into the *Critique of Pure Reason*, which after an hour or two of thoughtful study he returned to Henry.

"What was the score?" asked Henry, who was standing in the promenade, supervising the rigging of an exterior aluminum-foil sunshade to keep the blinding sunlight out of the promenade.

Dick shook his head. "Kant won by a knockout."

He watched the two crewmen working outside, clad in bulging space-suits. The ship was easing along on a sixteenth-gravity acceleration; a light cable connected them to a safety boom; magnetic slippers held them to the hull.

Beyond was emptiness. Dick craned his neck. Up, down, right, left: in all directions the black that was neither color nor density, the black that was nothing, and at a tremendous distance the blazing constellations. This was the elemental Gap, and it disturbed something deep in Dick's mind. He shuddered. "I'd hate to be lost out there."

"Yes," Henry admitted. "I would myself."

Dick watched the workers a moment. "Suppose the cable came loose."

"They'd drift astern, yelling bloody murder into their radios."

"And if their radios weren't working, and if no one saw them —"

"They'd be like men washed overboard at sea on a dark night. Done for."

Fascinated, Dick watched the crewmen rolling foil on to the standards. "Has it ever happened?"

"A few times, I suppose…I heard of a case where a man was lost behind, and picked up ten hours later, just before his oxygen gave out."

"And?"

"Brain like scrambled eggs. Crazy."

For a moment Dick was silent. Then he said, "A man might drift on the ocean for ten hours and still keep his sanity."

Henry shrugged. "Perhaps. If life began in the ocean as many believe, the memory would probably still be somewhere deep in our cells. But we've got nothing in our make-up to cope with space."

"I hope I never have to try," said Dick thoughtfully. "I can think of nicer ways to die."

"There aren't any nice ways to die," said Henry. "Some are worse than others. For instance —" he paused as Kirdy, the mate with the glossy mustache, came into the promenade.

"Henry, while you've got your men outside, it might be a good idea to string up the bridge awning too."

"Right," said Henry. He left the promenade and Dick returned to the lounge.

At a loss for occupation, he wrote a letter to his mother. His fellow passengers on the whole were rather dull people who spent hours playing cards or grouped around the ship's small bar. Sende, a notable exception, occupied himself striding around the promenade, falcon-head bent as if in thought, yellow eyes cold as lemons.

Ten days out from Venus they passed the halfway point. The ship twisted end for end, and acceleration became deceleration.

Three days afterward, Dick, climbing to the promenade, came upon Sende and Captain Henshaw under the ladder to the bridge. Sende was leaning forward, eyes glittering; Captain Henshaw stood like a bulldog with heavy jaws clenched.

Dick came to an abrupt halt. Sende gave him a quick glance, strode off with both Dick and the captain staring after him. Captain Henshaw muttered something incomprehensible, looked at Dick, started to speak, thought better of it, clamped his jaw shut. There was a moment of uncomfortable silence; then Captain Henshaw cleared his throat gruffly. "How are you enjoying the trip, Dick? A little monotonous, eh?"

"Well," said Dick carefully, "there's not much to do."

"That's bad, eh? You like excitement?"

Dick nodded. "I suppose I might as well make the most of it and be as lazy as I can, because as soon as I arrive on the moon my spare time ends."

"How's that? There's no school there."

"Well—" Dick hesitated, a little embarrassed. "I want to be an astronomer like my father, so once I'm at the observatory I'll probably have a lot of studying to do."

Captain Henshaw laughed. "I imagine your father puts you through it."

Dick grinned wryly. "He does when I don't catch on to things as fast as he thinks I ought to. Perhaps I don't have the right make-up. Sometimes I think I'd be a better explorer or detective."

Captain Henshaw looked down the promenade in the direction Sende had gone. "I wish you were a detective," he muttered. "There're a few people aboard I'd like to read a report on."

"I don't mean a criminal detective," said Dick. "I mean something more like a—well, I'm not quite sure. But I like to find out things. My father says I have too much curiosity for my own good."

Captain Henshaw chuckled. "He's wrong there; too much curiosity never hurt anyone. When a boy has too little, that's the time to start worrying."

"As a matter of fact," said Dick ingenuously, "I have a few questions I'd like to ask you."

The captain grimaced. "Very well. I let myself in for it. What's first?"

"First, why do we accelerate and decelerate so slowly? Couldn't we make a faster trip with more acceleration?"

"Indeed we could. After leaving Venus, if we accelerated at one Earth-gravity—that is, increased our speed 32 feet a second every second—for a day and a half, then decelerated at one gravity for another day and a half, we'd be on Earth. Sixty million miles in three days. But in such a case we'd use a great deal of expensive plutonium; we'd lose money on the trip. So we travel slower and use less power…What's the next question?"

"Well," said Dick hesitantly, "I've been wondering if you've heard from the *American Star*?"

Captain Henshaw answered shortly, "No."

"What do you think happened?"

Captain Henshaw looked out the window, scanned the glittering pageantry of the constellations. "As a matter of fact, I haven't any more facts at my disposal than you have."

Just then Kirdy jumped down from the bridge and floated slowly as a feather to the promenade. Captain Henshaw said frostily, "Someday you'll do that while we're on heavy gravity and break your neck."

"I was in a hurry, sir. Radar's picked up an object ahead."

"Why didn't you say so?" roared Captain Henshaw. He leaped for the bridge and Kirdy followed at his heels.

Dick heard the click of magnetic shoes; over his shoulder he saw Henry.

Henry paused, glanced into Dick's face. "You look as if you'd just seen a ghost. What's the trouble?"

Dick laughed uneasily. "No trouble that I know of. It's just that everyone is acting so strangely."

Henry made a noncommittal sound, went to the window, looked around the sky.

"You're doing it too," Dick observed pointedly. "What are you looking for?"

"I wish I knew."

"The mate reported a radar alarm and the captain was up on the bridge at one jump."

Henry asked with unusual sharpness, "Just now?"

"Just before you came. Why should the captain be so excited?"

"Because," said Henry grimly, "we're right in the middle of the Graveyard."

"The Graveyard?" Dick stared out into space, then back to Henry. "Why on earth —"

"Right here is where the *Canopus* and the *Capella* disappeared."

"I thought they were on the Mars run!"

"They'd still come right through here." Henry made a quick sketch on a sheet from his notebook. "That circle is the Graveyard. The last three ships to enter this circle disappeared without a trace."

"The last *three*?"

Henry looked uncomfortable. "The *American Star* was the third."

"But what's happening?"

Henry shrugged. "A good many people would like to know."

Kirdy looked down from the bridge. "Henry, the captain wants to see you."

Henry ran up the ladder. Dick waited, the back of his throat stiff with tension. He went to the window, looked out into space. Stars everywhere; everywhere the glinting multitudes… A thud behind him. Dick swung around, startled. Henry had jumped down from the bridge.

Dick opened his mouth to ask a question; Henry shook his head. "Can't stop to talk now." He started at a half-trot around the promenade.

Dick ran after him. "What have they picked up on the radar?"

"They think it's the *American Star.* Captain's ordered a lifeboat warmed up."

The promenade loud-speaker hummed; a voice spoke: "Attention personnel and passengers, prepare for heavy deceleration. Passengers will immediately take to their berths."

The message was repeated; Dick came to an indecisive halt. Henry looked over his shoulder. "Better get to your berth, Dick. We're slowing down awful sudden."

Dick reluctantly descended to his cabin; hardly had he stretched out when the deceleration pressed him against the mattress.

Uncomfortable hours passed. Dick tried to sleep, but excitement propped his eyelids wide, and his brain ran from idea to idea like an excited terrier. Why should the *American Star* be drifting out here in the middle of space? Why was Captain Henshaw unable to communicate across by radio? Certainly he would have tried. He must suspect something gravely wrong to decelerate from top speed in the middle of the voyage. Ten days acceleration, three days deceleration: that gave the effect of seven days acceleration at a sixteenth gravity, or seven-sixteenths of a day on one gravity, seven-thirty-seconds of a day or about five hours at two gravities. Add the initial two hours at two gravities, and the total was seven hours at two gravities, which now must be canceled to halt the *African Star*. Then they must return the distance by which they had overshot the *American Star*... So ran his thoughts.

Another hour dragged by; then for fifteen brief minutes the deceleration slacked while the stewardess, assisted by Henry and two of the crew, brought sandwiches and coffee to the passengers.

The pressure began again, and Dick fell into a doze. He suddenly came awake to find the weight gone from his chest. The speaker clicked, hummed. Captain Henshaw's voice said sharply, "Passengers please remain in your cabins; at any moment we may accelerate violently."

Dick rose to his knees, peered out the port. Black space and stars, Earth glowing ahead like an aquamarine on jeweler's velvet.

A scrape, a thump sounded along the hull; a spaceboat drifted away from the hull. Dick glimpsed Henry's serious dark face and Kirdy's marvellous mustache. Curiosity was too much for him. He took his binoculars, opened the door, looked out into the passage. No one in sight. He went quietly to the passengers' lounge, climbed to the promenade, looked in the direction the lifeboat had gone.

There it was, a glistening oval shape, gradually diminishing. Beyond, small in the distance, hung a spaceship, quiet, dark, dead.

Dick brought his binoculars to bear, set the magnification dial at 4, focused. The ship expanded; the profile became twin to that of the *African Star*. The ports were uniformly vacant, like the windows of a long-deserted house.

Dick steadied himself against the glass, dialed up the power. 6 — 8 — 10 — 12 — now any motion or tremor sent the field dancing wildly. Dick braced himself. 14 — 16 — 18. Even his pulse jarred the image.

The light scrape of footsteps sounded at his back. Dick whirled. Sende stood behind him, a faint grin on his face. "What do you see, young fellow?"

"The lifeboat is circling the ship," said Dick. "Aside from that —" he hesitated.

"No signs of life, eh?"

"No."

"Well, well." His expression was that of a man listening to far-off voices. Then his eyes seemed to focus on the present; he said politely, "Quite a serious affair, you might say."

"Yes, it certainly is."

"A tragedy even."

Dick glanced at him in surprise. "I suppose it must be."

"I wonder who is responsible."

"I have no idea. Do you?"

Sende pursed his lips as if he were whistling. "Maybe you've heard of the Basilisk?"

Dick considered. "Yes, somewhere; I can't quite remember. Who is it? Or is it a 'what'?"

Sende laughed softly. "If that question were answered, there might be an end to such things as—" he nodded toward the derelict. Dick twisted to look; when he turned back, Sende was striding easily around the promenade.

Dick raised his binoculars once more. The boat was on its way back to the ship. Dick descended to the lounge, crossed through the dining saloon, went out upon the lifeboat deck.

There was a metallic thump as the lifeboat slid home. Instantly Dick felt the pressure of acceleration under his feet—about half normal gravity.

The lock opened; Kirdy jumped into the room, his mustache bouncing. He gave Dick a swift cold glance, strode past, climbed the ladder. Henry came after, wiping the sweat from his forehead. He closed the port, reset the launching mechanism.

Dick asked, "What did you see?"

Henry shook his close-cropped head. "Kirdy says I'm not to talk." He darted a rather unfriendly glance up toward the bridge. "Personally," he muttered, "I don't see as it matters. Kirdy's got some strange notions, mighty strange notions."

"I saw the *American Star* through my binoculars," Dick told him. "It looked as if the bridge had been broken open."

Henry turned another glance up toward the bridge. "Kirdy calls it a meteor."

Dick laughed shortly. "Not unless the meteor exploded after entering the bridge. All the fragments are bent out, all the glass and metal.

It looked to me as if something — a rocket, say — had been fired into the hull."

Henry straightened up. "Just between you and me, that's about what happened. Inside the bridge —" he grimaced "— terrible. Bodies blown to bits. We looked into the promenade, and it was worse. The air blew out of the ship in one big puff, and the passengers — well, you might say they just popped open."

Dick swallowed hard. "But who fired the rocket — if it was a rocket?"

Henry was silent.

"Did you notice the cargo hold?"

"Open. Empty."

"Robbers," said Dick. "Pirates. Space pirates."

Henry nodded. "That's about it."

Dick asked, "Have you ever heard of the Basilisk?"

Henry looked up. "What about the Basilisk?"

"I asked you."

Henry said in a low voice, "There're rumors. I didn't put much stock in them before."

Dick waited. After a moment Henry said, "They go to the effect that the Basilisk rules space, and any ship that trespasses he claims as his own."

"That's fantastic!"

"Fantastic or not, he's already blown open three ships that we know of and made off with millions of dollars worth of cargo. He's killed hundreds of men and women, a merciless devil. It's hard to think of him as human."

"And what happens to the ships? Have they ever found the *Canopus* or the *Capella*?"

"No. I've got a hunch that the Basilisk puts a prize crew aboard, takes them to his base, repairs them, installs weapons."

"But the *American Star*..."

Henry shrugged. "I imagine he transshipped the cargo, and got that safe first. If this business follows the same pattern as the *Canopus* and the *Capella*, he'll be back to pick up the *American Star* and add it to his fleet."

Dick scanned the sky anxiously. "He might be following us now."

"It's possible enough. Captain Henshaw's been on pins and needles."

After a moment Dick asked, "Where did you hear all this about the Basilisk?"

Henry chewed his lip thoughtfully. "As a matter of fact, Kirdy told me."

Dick ruminated further. "But where does the Basilisk take all these ships? He'd need big shops, machinery, supplies."

Henry glanced up into space, past the red glare of Mars to the massive white light that was Jupiter. "Kirdy claims that he's got a base out on one of the Jovian satellites."

The loud-speaker hummed. The voice — Kirdy's voice — spoke: "Passengers may now leave their cabins. We will continue on the present acceleration until we are back on schedule."

"If I were a detective," said Dick thoughtfully, "I'd ask Kirdy some questions."

But six hours later Kirdy was past the reach of any mortal inquisition. His body was found on the promenade under the bridge, his neck broken, the back of his head almost resting on his chest.

Captain Henshaw, looking from the limp form to the hole into the bridge, said, "I told the young fool he'd break his neck someday."

# CHAPTER III

## *Ghostly Ruins*

A VOICE LIKE METAL scraping metal said, "Now what are you up to, young fellow?" Dick twisted sharply. Sende stood behind him. It seemed one of Sende's characteristics to be always where you expected him least, and Dick found it unnerving.

He said, "I was thinking that a man jumping down from the bridge would be more likely to break his legs than his neck."

Sende's blank yellow eyes seemed to hide intricate inner processes. He said softly, "That's an interesting idea. What's your theory?"

Dick said lamely, "I don't have any theory. I was just noticing—"

From the bridge came an angry mutter, then the thud of footsteps. Captain Henshaw climbed down the ladder, his jaw set at a challenging angle.

Sende asked lazily, "What's the trouble, Captain?"

"No trouble," barked Captain Henshaw. "No trouble! Just that we're in the middle of the Graveyard with heaven only knows what likely to happen, and now the radar and radio take the notion to go out, and Kirdy the radioman dead. If anything happened, we couldn't see it coming, we couldn't even call for help!"

Sende shook his head. "Disturbing."

"Disturbing!" roared Captain Henshaw. "It's sabotage! The instruments were going smooth as cream yesterday."

Dick said hesitantly, "I know a little about radios."

Captain Henshaw laughed bitterly. "You keep your hands off. First thing I know you'd electrocute yourself and I'd have two corpses on my hands." He stamped around the promenade.

Dick glanced at Sende and was surprised to see the knife-slit mouth twisted into a faint smile. Dick said dryly, "You don't seem too upset about Kirdy's death or at the prospect of pirates killing us all."

Sende's grin widened. "Pirates? Now where did you fish up that notion?"

"Why, it's common knowledge. The Basilisk..."

"Superstition," scoffed Sende. He gestured out into space. "Look out there — billions and billions of cubic miles. How could a pirate hope to find a ship in all that?"

"Well," said Dick, "he might know the ship's course; or he could trace the ship's radio." He fell silent.

Sende nodded. "Maybe it's a good thing the radio is quiet, eh?"

Dick reluctantly agreed. "But I still would like to know about Kirdy's broken neck."

Sende said in a confidential voice, "I'll tell you a secret. Kirdy was a heavy drinker. He probably went on watch tipsy and fell down the ladder."

"After smashing the radio and radar, I suppose?"

"It's possible. As reasonable as pirates." And Sende went on around the promenade.

The days passed without further incident. Earth swelled, became a great green and blue ball, streaked over with feathery wisps of clouds. To the side hung the moon, black, silver, white and gray; pocked with craters, scarred and scabbed, a world as different from Earth as death is from life.

On the twentieth day out from Venus the *African Star* went into an orbit a hundred miles above the surface of the moon, coasting at a speed just sufficient, by virtue of the centrifugal force so generated, to balance the moon's gravity. Dick stood on the promenade observing the haunted and desolate surface through his glasses. "How do I get down to the observatory?" he asked Henry. "Does the ship land?"

Henry laughed. "Captain Henshaw would drop you on a parachute before he'd use up the fuel it takes to land."

"I'd hit the ground pretty hard without any air for the parachute."

"Makes no difference; the captain likes to show a profit for the voyage."

"But how do I get down?"

"Well, there's no Heaviside layer on the moon, so radio waves won't go around the horizon as they do on Earth. But as soon as we coast to where we can see the observatory, Captain Henshaw will radio down for the dispatch boat."

"Radio? I thought the radio was out of commission."

"One of the passengers fixed it. I don't know who; I was off watch at the time."

Dick packed his binoculars back into their case. "I suppose I'd better get my luggage together." He descended the staircase to the cabin deck; with the ship coasting freely in orbit there was neither acceleration nor gravity, and he found it necessary to pull himself downstairs.

Ten minutes later he closed the door to Berth 22 for the last time, walked on magnetic slippers down the passage, floating his bags ahead of him. He descended the staircase to the chamber behind the exit port, herded his bags into a corner.

He heard magnetic slippers behind him; Sende entered and pushed his bags into the corner beside Dick's.

Dick stared dumfounded. "Are you landing on the moon?" he asked lamely.

Sende's yellow eyes were blank as pebbles. "Any reason why I shouldn't?"

"No," said Dick hastily, "of course not. But you never mentioned —"

"Neither did you."

"Well, no," Dick had to admit. He looked glumly through the port-hole. Sende's presence was not a pleasant surprise. Dick sighed, made a mental adjustment. Sende, after all, was nothing to him, one way or the other. "I suppose you're going to the observatory?"

Sende had been watching him with a fixed, rather dead, smile. "There's nowhere else to go since the Security Station shut down. The moon's a quiet place nowadays."

"Are you planning to stay long?" Dick asked hopefully.

Sende nodded. "Quite a long time."

"Oh! Then you must be an astronomer."

"No. That's a long way out of my line. I'm a radio operator."

Dick once more found himself staring at Sende. "Then," he blurted out, "why didn't you fix the ship's radio?"

"I did," replied Sende composedly. "Finished yesterday, just in time to call down for the dispatch boat."

He looked out the bull's-eye. "And here it comes now."

Outside, the oval dome of the little craft glinted in the sunlight. Four blasts of blue flame slanted down and back. The jets flickered, dimmed; the boat slid on up paralleling the orbit of the *African Star*, drifting close. A moment later there came a soft thud as it touched the hull; in another moment the ports met and sealed. Henry swung the door back; a small Japanese with a good-humored expression jumped into the ship. With a trace of disappointment, Dick saw that his father was not aboard.

The Japanese looked from Dick to Sende, then back to Dick. "You're Dick Murdock?"

"Yes."

"I'm John Terenabe. Your father couldn't meet the ship, but you'll be seeing him in an hour." He turned to Sende, nodded. "You must be my replacement."

"Correct. If you're the radio operator."

"I am. I think you'll find work at the observatory very congenial." He stood aside as Dick pushed his bags through the port. "You can fly one of these boats?" he asked Sende.

Sende nodded.

"Good," said Terenabe. "I've been meeting the ships; no doubt you'll inherit the job."

Sende pushed his own bags in after Dick's.

Captain Henshaw appeared, shook hands with Sende, who ducked through the porthole, took a seat in the boat. The captain turned to Dick. "Now, Dick, behave yourself, and keep that lump of curiosity under some kind of control."

Dick laughed. "I can't guarantee anything, Captain."

Captain Henshaw held out his hand. "Maybe we'll see each other again, Dick."

"I hope so." Dick turned to Henry. "So long, Henry." They shook hands; Dick slipped through the lock. The port thudded behind him. Terenabe slammed the boat's port, unhooked the grapples.

With a lump in his throat, Dick watched the great hull drift away. Both the ship and the dispatch boat changed course; the ship dwindled across the gulf, became a glinting spot, was lost.

The boat slanted down toward the moon with the sun low astern. Jagged mountains cast fantastic black shadows across the lunar plains; the innumerable craters showed as alternate bright crescents and ovals of shade.

"Well," said Sende, "what do you think of it?"

Dick shook his head. "There's too much to think about. I suppose it's beautiful, except 'beautiful' isn't really the right word."

Terenabe looked over his shoulder. "It's something you never get used to, no matter how long you stay out here."

The boat dropped lower; Earth rose over the horizon, an enormous globe three-quarters full. Asia and the Pacific Ocean were visible with the North Pole at the bottom, as if Earth were standing on its head.

Terenabe's voice broke in on Dick's thoughts. "We're coming to the old Security Station."

Dick shifted in his seat. "Where?"

Terenabe pointed. Dick brought out his binoculars, focused. "I've heard the Security Station mentioned, but I don't remember much about it."

"It's a relic of the bad old days," said Terenabe, "when dictators and slave states threatened the free people of the world."

"It was one of the first acts of the United Nations, wasn't it?"

"Well, not quite the first. One of the first decisive acts, you might say. When the first spaceships left the Earth — long before your time — the United Nations decided to build a great fort here on the moon. There were hangars with atom rockets guided by television, radioactive dusts — the most terrible weapons ever conceived. No nation, no matter how militaristic and aggressive, dared to threaten war. The United Nations, which had been unable to join nations together in peace, was suddenly strong enough to impose peace."

"It doesn't look very imposing now."

"It's no longer needed. The dictators lost their followings, the slave states broke up. There were no longer armies or threats of war on Earth, so the Security Station was abandoned. The personnel went home, the weapons were scrapped, the bombs were converted to fuel for spaceships. The barracks and general headquarters were blown up as a symbolic gesture, and the ruins remain as you see them."

"It seems rather a waste," said Dick. "Still, I suppose a fort is good for nothing except just being a fort."

"Not a thing in the world," said Terenabe. "If the dictators and militarists who used to start wars had to earn by manual labor what their wars cost, there would have been very few wars." He looked down at the desolate ruins passing below: runways, blockhouses, piers, hangars, docks, warehouses, barracks, gleaming white and eery. "We still use the old radio transmitter to broadcast trans-space messages — all entirely automatic, of course. Signals from the observatory are relayed to the Station and then beamed to Earth."

"Isn't that rather inconvenient?" asked Dick. "Suppose the equipment breaks down?"

Terenabe shook his head. "Security Station equipment was built so it wouldn't break down. The system works; there has never been any reason to move the transmitter to the observatory, so there it stays."

Dick studied the Station through his binoculars. He said with an uncertain laugh, "It looks haunted — like an ancient abandoned city. I could almost picture ghosts walking in a place like that."

Terenabe chuckled. "You've got quite an imagination, Dick."

Dick leaned forward, fingers twisting the magnification dial.

"What's the trouble?"

"I thought you said the Station was deserted."

"So it is. There's a caretaker, but he never goes near the place."

"I saw a light," said Dick.

Sende, who had been listening with aloof and sardonic amusement, said suddenly, "Let's see." He took the binoculars, peered down at the white ruins now drifting astern. After a moment he said, "No, just reflection on glass."

"But —" Dick's voice trailed off. Impatiently he waited for Sende to return his binoculars so that he might check on his observation, but Sende seemed in no hurry to relinquish them. He studied the old

Station critically, then swept the harsh panorama to all sides. When he handed back the glasses the Station was far astern.

After a few minutes Terenabe said, "See that crater wall ahead?"

"Yes. There's something on top, something glittering like metal."

"That's the big telescope." He frowned for a reason which Dick at the moment did not comprehend. "On the other side of the crater is the observatory."

# CHAPTER IV

## The Killer Eye

THE BOAT SETTLED DOWN into the crater. In the slanting sunlight the buildings of the observatory looked little different from the modern concrete buildings of Earth or Venus, except that the windows were smaller and fewer and all the flat surfaces bulged outward.

Dick said with a trace of disappointment, "I thought there was a dome over the entire observatory."

"No," said Terenabe. "Those domes figured a great deal in early speculation, but when the engineers got to work they built conventional buildings — especially reinforced against air pressure, of course." He pointed to the largest of the buildings, a structure three stories high. "That's the administration building, with the laboratories at the rear. That big round building is our garden; we grow all our fruit and vegetables in hydroponic tanks. Then there's the dormitory and mess hall, the electrolysis plant and the machine shop. The atomic pile and generator are on the other side of old Killer, under the crater wall —"

"'Killer'?" asked Dick.

Terenabe hesitated. "That's what we call the big telescope. You'll hear all about it from your father." He hurried on. "You can see the road leading out to the ice mine —" He smiled at the expression on Dick's face. "Does that sound strange to you?"

Dick nodded, "I'm afraid it does."

Terenabe patted the controls of the boat. "That's what you're flying on. Ice."

"I guess I'm dense. I don't understand how anyone can fly on ice."

Terenabe laughed. "Well, these boats are too small to use atomic energy. Freighting fuel out from Earth is expensive. So we mine ice from a vein laid down while the moon was cooling, melt it, break it down into hydrogen and oxygen by passing electricity through it."

"In the electrolysis plant. Now I see."

"The oxygen and hydrogen are stored outside in tanks, where they liquefy in the absolute-zero cold. And that's the fuel we're burning now." Terenabe looked down at the observatory, now only five hundred feet below. "And I think I see your father — there, in that blue space-suit."

The crags of the crater wall rose past the ship; the telescope, catching the sunlight, gleamed against the black sky.

The boat touched ground. The man in the blue space-suit ran up; through the head dome Dick distinguished the face of his father.

Terenabe waved. "Now," he said, "we wait till they bring up the bird cage. Here it comes."

Two men trundled the odd vehicle across the crater floor: a globe mounted on two light wheels. They maneuvered it against the entrance port, tightened down the sealing flange.

Terenabe opened the port. "Okay, let's go. Bring your bags."

Dick waved once more at his father, carried his bags into the globe. The doors shut, he felt himself being wheeled across the flat.

A moment later the ball stopped. Once again they heard the sound of the seal-rings, then the port opened. "All out," cried Terenabe. "You're here, end of the line."

Dick stepped into a room like the lobby of a small but expensive hotel. "This is the recreation lounge," said Terenabe. "And here comes your father; I'll leave the rest of the explaining to him."

Observatory personnel numbered sixty, ranging from Dr. Murdock through senior and junior astronomers, technicians, laboratory assistants, mechanics, bookkeepers, a doctor, an electrician, a librarian, a radio operator, commissary and dormitory staff, two gardeners, a few miscellaneous workers. There were men of all ages and every regional background, from Isel Bayer, the wispy old librarian with dark glasses and white hair fluffy as sugar floss, to Mervin Hutchings, a weedy youth with a long pinched face, only a few years older than Dick.

Second in authority was Professor Frederick Dexter. He had brilliant and compelling black eyes in a rather grim white face and carried himself with iron erectness. Dick got the impression of great vitality under rigid control.

After the twentieth handshake, the twentieth "Glad to know you, Dick," faces and names ceased to connect themselves. Dr. Murdock noticed the lack of enthusiasm in Dick's responses. "Are you tired?"

Dick considered. "Yes, I suppose so."

"Like to take a nap?"

"It's the middle of the day, isn't it?"

Dr. Murdock shrugged. "Day and night don't mean much here; we more or less sleep when we feel in the mood."

"I'm tired," said Dick, "but I'm — well, excited at the same time."

His father looked at his watch. "It's just after our breakfast time. Suppose you sleep till two; then there'll be time for us to make the rounds before Sundown Supper."

"Sundown Supper? What's that?"

His father grinned. "Just an excuse for a big feed. Once every month the sun sets, and we mark the occasion with fried chicken and strawberry shortcake with whipped cream. Two weeks later we have Sunrise Breakfast, and then we have strawberry waffles with whipped cream. Keeps Doc Mole busy."

"And who is Doc Mole?"

"He's the cook — a good man to stay on the right side of." Dr. Murdock laughed. "He heard young Hutchings grumbling about his food; and last sundown Hutch got a wing and a neck; then there was some real grumbling. Come along, I'll show you your room. We'll have to bunk together; the observatory is rather pinched for space."

They climbed a metal staircase; Dr. Murdock paused on the second-floor landing. "Down there," he pointed to the right, "is the library and the photography shop, which is Professor Dexter's specialty. And down there — to the left — are the general offices: bookkeeping, payroll and the like. There's lots of paperwork to a big place like this. I'm an astronomer only about half the time; the other half I'm a combination banker, father-confessor, cattle wrangler, referee, nose wiper —"

Dick laughed. One of his father's most admirable qualities, so he considered, was an easy tolerance of annoyances which might have driven other men to distraction.

"And there," said Dr. Murdock, pointing to a white door painted with a red cross, "that's the dispensary. Now we'll proceed to the third floor, where there's nothing more exciting than living quarters."

Dr. Murdock's suite consisted of a corner bedroom, a small office and bath. "We'll bring in a bed for you after supper. You can use those drawers and that half of the closet."

Dick had been examining the naked steel girder at the corner of the room. "Seems like terrifically heavy construction."

"It has to be. Figure it out for yourself. That end of the room is fifteen feet wide by eight high: 120 square feet. In square inches that's about — let's see — 144, call it 150, times 120 is 12,000 plus 6,000, 18,000. Knock off a thousand, call it 17,000 square inches. We keep the air pressure at thirteen pounds per square inch." He scribbled on the back of an envelope. "That's one hundred and ten tons pushing against that one section of wall alone. The engineers did a lot of careful work designing these buildings — working with forces they never need to consider on Earth."

Dick was looking out the little round window. "It doesn't open," said his father. "You don't go leaning out for a breath of fresh air here on the moon." He sank into a chair. "Now suppose you tell me about your trip."

Dick took a seat, described the events of the voyage. When he had finished, his father rubbed his chin. "You speak of Sende as if you had something against him."

Dick hesitated. "Not really. There's nothing I can put my finger on. I just have a funny feeling about him, as if he's posing, playing some kind of part."

"He's an extraordinary-looking chap," remarked Dr. Murdock thoughtfully. "His face doesn't give anything away. But he came to the job with the highest recommendations, and naturally if he does his work well, we can't be prejudiced by his appearance."

"No, I suppose not," said Dick. "But I have an idea, intuition I suppose you'd call it, that he knows more about Kirdy's death than he let on."

His father shrugged. "Well, we'll keep an eye on him." He glanced at his watch. "You'd better take your nap now."

Dick awoke at one-thirty, dressed, ran downstairs, where he found his father, and they set out on the tour of the observatory.

The four main buildings were mutually interjoined by tubular metal passageways. Starting around in a counterclockwise direction, they came out into a large round hall like a saucer turned upside down. Arched girders and crystal panes made a geometric pattern overhead; below was an ordered profusion of vegetation in long shallow tanks.

Dr. Murdock said proudly, "We grow everything you can think of, from potatoes to grapes; our main problem is eating it all. Also, as you must know, plants absorb carbon dioxide and give off oxygen; and this greenhouse handles three-quarters of our air purification." He pointed to the ceiling. "Notice the drains running under the girders? The water vapor which is evaporated from the plants, and also from our lungs, condenses against the cold panes, trickles down into the drains, back into the hydroponic tanks. We're almost self-sufficient here."

"It must take lots of energy for heat and light."

Dr. Murdock nodded. "I don't know what we'd do without the atomic pile. We could hardly haul enough fuel out from Earth to keep us going. Well, let's get on; there's a lot to see. We won't bother with the mess hall; we'll cut right around to the electrolysis plant."

Halfway along the tube he stopped, pointed through a small circular peephole to a tall metal structure. "There's the ice bin, and below is the ice wagon."

Dick asked, "What are those big shiny cones?"

"Reflectors. We melt the ice by solar heat; the reflectors focus sunlight. Here on the moon, without air, dust, clouds to act as a screen, the sunlight is pretty fierce. You can't go bareheaded out into the sunlight." He considered his words, chuckled. "You can't even go bareheaded out in the dark, unless you're tired of life. But what I meant is that you've got to shield your eyes and skin, otherwise you'd have the worst case of sunburn and sun blindness you can imagine." He sobered suddenly. "Sunlight is very dangerous around here."

They continued into the electrolysis plant. With fascination Dick watched water in the bank of U-shaped tubes disintegrating into oxygen and hydrogen. As soon as they were formed, the gases were pumped away, first to liquefy in the exterior cold, then to storage tanks.

"Now," said Dr. Murdock, "back to the administration building for space-suits, and then we'll go out to the big telescope."

Dick remembered the term Terenabe had used. "Why do you call it the 'Killer'?"

Dr. Murdock screwed up his face. "So it's got to you already. Well, hold your horses, I'll tell you all about it as soon as we get up there."

He glanced out the window. "Hello, old Sam Baxter is with us again. See that contraption?"

Dick, coming to the window, saw a rickety-looking framework ten feet long by four feet wide. Outriggers extended across either end; the device resembled the letter *I*, with the vertical stroke representing the platform, the serifs the outriggers. Each outrigger terminated in a battered and corroded jet on a universal joint. Two benches were fixed to the platform; underneath were two large tanks. In front was a rude control panel bristling with valves and handles.

"What is it?" asked Dick.

"That's Crazy Sam's raft." He cocked a sidewise glance at Dick. "I suppose I shouldn't call him Crazy Sam, but I hear it so often it seems part of his name."

"Who is Crazy Sam?"

"Well, in theory he's caretaker at the old Security Station; but I doubt if he ever sets foot in the place. He seems to spend his time drifting around the moon on that raft, doing a little prospecting, a little digging. I'd better warn you — don't get on his bad side; he's a cantankerous old duffer and holds onto grudges as if they were his teeth."

"But why do they call him 'Crazy'?" Dick asked.

"Oh," his father made a vague gesture, "he subscribes to a belief that there's a race of lunar natives, that they live in deep caves where there's still air and a little internal heat."

"And you don't believe him?"

Dr. Murdock smiled. "I haven't seen any evidence to support his ideas. I'm afraid I'm a little skeptical."

They came to the main building. "This way," said Dr. Murdock. "We'll get into our space-suits."

"Hey Doc," came a loud voice, harsh as a parrot screech.

Dr. Murdock stopped short, made a wry face at Dick, turned slowly. "Hello, Sam. How goes it?"

A little man with parched brown skin and a big head came erratically across the room. He hopped sidewise like a bird, making frequent little starts and stops and small darts to the side. Coming to a sudden halt he stood staring from Dr. Murdock to Dick with crafty gray eyes. He spoke, filling the air with jerky little gestures. "Not too glad to see me, eh? Afraid I'll upset some of your nice schoolbook theories? Well, that's all right. I say a man's got a right to his own beliefs, and if nobody else likes it, they can go dive into Aristillus Crater...And who's the young sprout? Hey boy, ain't you got a tongue?"

"Allow me to introduce my son," said Dr. Murdock gravely. "Sam Baxter — Dick."

"How do you do," Dick politely started to say, but his new acquaintance interrupted him before he had passed the first word.

"Call me Crazy Sam, boy; everyone else does, and I take it as a compliment. Because I knows what I knows, and I see what I see, and if nobody else knows and sees — why, so much the better...Now, what's my name?"

Dick hesitated an uncomfortable second. "Well, Crazy Sam if you like, but I'd want to form my own opinion of your sanity. Maybe you're right and everybody else is wrong."

Crazy Sam gave vent to an ear-splitting cackle of laughter. "Boy, you've said the first sensible thing I've heard since Hector was a pup." He turned back to Dr. Murdock. "Now look here, Doc, I thought you was going to tell Lobscouse or whatever his name is to allow me all the fuel I needed."

Dr. Murdock smote his forehead. "Sam, I clean forgot. I'll tell him at suppertime. You'll be staying of course."

"Of course. Where else do I go? To the Ritz-Carlton around the corner? Or maybe the Savoy Grill out on Mare Serenitatis?"

He hopped off grumbling to himself. Dr. Murdock, looking after him, shook his head ruefully. He turned back to Dick. "Well, we've got to hurry."

Ten minutes later, clad in space-suits, they crossed the crater floor—black glass deep and clear as sea water. Behind, the buildings of the observatory stood sharp and brilliant in the full flat light of the sun. After the golden haze and mellow distances of Venus, Dick found it hard to get used to the uncompromising starkness of the lunar scene. Outlines, bulks, shadows, details twenty miles away were as painfully distinct as those under his feet; it gave the landscape a puzzling complexity, a peculiar foreshortening as if normal perspective was lacking.

Ahead rose the crater wall: gray, white and black crags, splintered prisms with fracture-planes gleaming like mirrors, steeper and harsher than any of the great Venus ranges. The top of a low bluff had been blasted to provide a foundation for the telescope. Complex as lace it stood on the black sky, bright metal glistening in the sunlight, and for all its intricacy it seemed somehow more substantial than the lunar mountains themselves. The mirror hung at the bottom of the trusswork tube; almost at the top was the observer's cage, dwarfed in comparison with the mirror.

Dr. Murdock was peering into Dick's helmet; his lips were moving in a peculiar fashion. Suddenly Dick realized he was speaking, but naturally enough, with a vacuum intervening, he was unable to hear. Dr. Murdock stepped over, touched a switch on Dick's belt. A hum sounded in Dick's ears as the radio warmed up; he heard his father's voice grow out of nothing, reach normal pitch.

"We don't have a very good path up to the Eye; in this weak gravity it's easier to jump than to walk. But be careful, don't overshoot."

He led the way up, rising in effortless bounds; presently they stood beside the telescope.

Dick inspected the immaculate face of the mirror with awed admiration. It seemed as wide as the floor of a house. "How did they ever build a thing this big and bring it up here without breaking it? It must be thirty feet across."

His father laughed. "Thirty-six feet. And the mirror was constructed right here."

"But how in the world—"

"The engineers employed a very ingenious process; the mirror is actually solid quicksilver. It was poured as a liquid into the rim casing, which was then rotated very slowly. Centrifugal force pressed the quicksilver out against the rim of the casing in a perfect uniform curve. After a moment the quicksilver congealed, froze into shape."

"You could build a mirror as big as you wanted — any size!" marvelled Dick.

Dr. Murdock nodded. "Theoretically, yes. Killing the vibration is the hardest part, since the slightest tremor flaws the mirror. Every last little rasp and drag has to be eliminated; the quicksilver is even shielded from dust. The casing pivoted on a piston only an inch in diameter in a pool of oil; the torque is supplied magnetically. As a result, we have the most powerful instrument human ingenuity can conceive. And, of course, out here we have perfect seeing."

"There really aren't any limits as to how far you can see now, are there?"

Dr. Murdock smiled, shook his head wistfully. "We still have limits, of a different kind. In the old days on Earth we had air currents, haze, reflected atmospheric light, the weight of the mirror itself to contend with. Out here the mirror weighs one-seventh as much as it would on Earth. Air can't blur our vision because there isn't any air; an object is above the horizon for two weeks, which gives us almost unlimited time for photographic exposures. Now the delicacy and detail of our seeing is limited by the accuracy of the drive, which swings the telescope across the sky to follow a star, the grain of our photographic plates, and cosmic haze — the stray molecules out in space. Still we've already looked out a hundred times farther than was possible with the old Palomar reflector."

Dick regarded the telescope with enormous respect. "But why do they call it the Killer?"

Dr. Murdock appeared a little uncomfortable. "The chief astronomer before me was Dr. Vrosnek, a great scientist. The telescope killed him in a freak accident, which we hope," he said in a subdued voice, "will never happen again." He pointed to a metal parasol. "That's the sun-shield. Whenever a man is working in the cage, that shield is adjusted to shadow the mirror from the sun. Because if, by some mistake or neglect, the telescope were pointed at the sun without the shield, the sunlight focusing inside the cage would burn the observer and all his instruments to a cinder. That, regrettably, is what happened to Dr. Vrosnek. By some strange oversight —" he repeated the words thoughtfully "— a very strange oversight, he neglected to use the sun-shield, and he was burned to death."

Dick shuddered. "I suppose it was quick enough."

"Yes, mercifully."

"And then you were appointed Chief Astronomer?"

"Yes. It was perhaps a little unfair to Professor Dexter, who was on the spot, but the trustees nominated me. And so," he held out his hands, "here we are."

Dick's mind had reverted to the incidents of the voyage. "Could you see a spaceship leave Earth?"

"Easily. We could follow it all the way to Venus."

"The pirates would find a telescope like this handy."

Dr. Murdock was silent for several minutes. At last he said: "It's certainly obvious that they can't rely upon chance to find their victims. Space is too big. I can think of only two ways they could operate. They could place a confederate aboard the ship they intended to plunder, either as a passenger or as a member of the crew. Or they could arrange to have access to a telescope like this one."

Dick looked uneasily from the telescope to the buildings of the observatory below, out to the lonely reaches of the lunar landscape. "They might even land men behind the crater, kill us all and take control of the observatory."

Dr. Murdock laughed. "I suppose it's possible…"

Their headphones clicked open to a new voice. "Dr. Murdock, we've sighted a strange ship; it seems to be armed and it's coming down toward the observatory!"

# CHAPTER V

## *Pirate Fever*

DR. MURDOCK AND DICK turned with one accord to scan the sky. With a thumping heart Dick pointed. "Look…" Dr. Murdock gazed upward; in silence they watched the strange ship. It was smaller than the trans-space passenger packets, but proportionately longer. A peculiar long bridge across the blunt bow gave it the appearance of a clumsy but dangerous hammerhead shark.

Dick saw his father jerk as if arousing himself from a kind of spell. "If that actually is a pirate ship, we're through." He started downhill. "We can't fight; there's nothing here more dangerous than Doc Mole's butcher knives."

Dick hesitated a moment, squinting up at the hull. It was settling across the sunlight; details were hard to see. Then the ship turned slightly, and Dick glimpsed a blue insignia. His heart gave a quick bound. "It's a UN ship," he cried out. "I see the emblem."

Dr. Murdock halted, peered up at the hull. "Yes, I see now." He growled, "They should know better than to give us a scare like that."

The ship landed on the black glass of the crater floor. The port swung open and three men in space-suits jumped to the ground.

Dr. Murdock went across to meet them. Dick came a few feet behind, the thought occurring to him that anyone, pirate or not, could paint a UN emblem on his ship. The man in the lead had a calm, blunt face, and he spoke with a calm, blunt voice exactly suited to his face. Dick's suspicions vanished. No pirate would speak so matter-of-factly; pirates by their very nature were dramatic and flamboyant. "I'm Commander Joseph Franchetti; I'd like to speak to Dr. Murdock."

"I'm Dr. Murdock." Dick's father looked a little sourly at the ship. "You might have given us warning. We're suffering from pirate fever; you scared us all out of a year's growth."

Franchetti grinned. "Sorry, but we're here to talk about pirates, and I didn't want to broadcast our whereabouts across the whole Solar System."

Dr. Murdock nodded. "Well, come along inside and we'll talk in comfort. We're just about to eat supper; perhaps you'll join us?"

"Delighted. Glad for a change from navy chow."

Dr. Murdock glanced from the collar of Franchetti's gray-blue uniform, barely visible under the helmet, to the ship. "Navy?"

Franchetti glanced back at his ship. "Not too imposing, is it? That's the UN Space Navy — half of it. The corvette *Theseus*. The corvette *Achilles* is the other half. But there's more on the way."

They turned toward the administration building, with Franchetti's two companions following close behind. Dick inspected them curiously. They were enough alike to be brothers, with long inquisitive noses, careful black eyes, bony chins.

Inside the administration building, with the space-suits off, Franchetti introduced his companions. "Mr. Millbank and Mr. Chain, of the Tri-World Insurance Corporation." He looked at them with a glint of humor. "They're very much concerned by the losses their company has suffered through the pirates."

"My son Dick," said Dr. Murdock in turn, "and here is Professor Dexter. Suppose we have our supper here in the lounge where we can talk a little more freely, instead of the mess hall." He went to the telephone, called instructions to the steward.

Commander Franchetti glanced appreciatively around the lounge. "Nice place you have here, Doctor. Deep leather couches, window boxes full of geraniums — almost like home."

Dr. Murdock laughed. "We're completely practical. It's necessary to sit somewhere, so we have couches. The geraniums are not only decorative but they give off a great deal of oxygen."

Two stewards in white coats set up a table. While they were waiting for dinner, Dr. Murdock said, "Dick here has probably been closer to the pirates than any one of us."

"How's that?" asked Franchetti, while Millbank and Chain inspected Dick with wary interest.

"He arrived from Venus on the *African Star*. Along the way, as you probably know, they passed the hulk of the *American Star*."

"Well, well. You must have felt rather exposed, Dick."

"I didn't feel too comfortable after looking at the wreck they made of the bridge."

"There were eighty-five men and women killed in that one ship," Franchetti mused. "Add ninety in the *Canopus* and seventy-two in the *Capella*; you have almost two hundred and fifty persons murdered in the coldest of cold blood. The Basilisk—" Franchetti accented the word wryly "—is a devil with acid in his veins."

"He's cost our company millions," said Millbank with intense feeling. "Detestable, a terrible person." And Chain nodded in complete agreement.

Professor Dexter said, "There must be symbolism of some sort in the name 'Basilisk', but I find it incomprehensible."

Dick's father rubbed his chin. "Perhaps because he inspires such terror; no, that's a little lame."

Professor Dexter shook his head. "The Basilisk—fantastic! Fantastic that we can sit here discussing pirates as calmly as if they were hit-and-run drivers!"

"For a fact," admitted Franchetti, "it does seem a little rich. About five hundred years out of style, along with galleons and the Spanish Main."

"When you consider the matter in broad perspective," said Professor Dexter, "we have today conditions almost identical to those which produced the pirates of the sixteenth and seventeenth centuries: unprotected ships carrying valuable cargoes, poor communications, no adequate police force. Given the same conditions, and given human nature, it's almost inevitable that the result should be the same."

"Just what is being done in regard to adequate policing, Commander?" asked Dr. Murdock.

Franchetti shook his head grimly. "Too little. The *Theseus* is only two months old, the *Achilles* won't be in commission for another week. There's a heavy cruiser on the ways which probably will be able to deal handily with the pirates, but she can't be in action for another year."

"And in the meantime?"

"In the meantime — the spaceships take their chances or they stay in port."

"But they can't stay in port; Venus and Mars would be isolated!"

Franchetti shrugged. "That's what the Basilisk is counting on; that's where he'll cash in."

"If I recall correctly," said Professor Dexter, "it's precisely what happened in the Old Caribbean. And when pickings at sea grew too slim, the pirates raided cities along the coast, and the slaughter was even worse than it was at sea."

Dick had a sudden vivid picture in his mind: roaring bestial men in the calm streets of Miracle Valley, burning, destroying, carrying off women...Who could stop them? Who, even, could stop them from raiding the observatory and killing the lot of them? He shuddered. Franchetti noticed. "A little sticky, eh, Dick?"

"I didn't think human beings nowadays were quite that cruel."

His father said in a bitter voice that Dick rarely heard him use: "Give the human race time, Dick. It's still very young, still very close to brutality."

Millbank cleared his throat in order to bring the conversation back to its proper channels. "Naturally, Dr. Murdock, we are very concerned. There are over twenty ships in the interplanetary trade, most of them insured by us. If the Basilisk —" he pronounced the word as if it were an indecency "— destroys many more, our company will be seriously embarrassed."

"Naturally I understand your position," said Dr. Murdock, "but why have you come to us here at the observatory?"

"Because you operate one of the few devices that might help us track down the killers."

"I suppose you refer to the telescope."

"Exactly."

"My son and I," Dr. Murdock continued reflectively, "were only an hour ago discussing the fact that the pirates must either have a confederate aboard the ship they intend to loot or else must be able to observe the ship's movements for sufficient time to calculate its correct speed, direction and acceleration. I know of only one place where he could do all this—here at the observatory."

"Exactly. And by the same token, we should be able to follow the Basilisk to his base, if we ever caught a glimpse of him."

"I agree, but how could we catch this glimpse?"

"You might keep an eye on ships passing through the Graveyard; then if the Basilisk attacks, you've got him fair and square, in the middle of the lens."

Dr. Murdock frowned dubiously, "Well, I don't know. What do you think, Dexter?"

Professor Dexter shrugged. "It's worth a try, but as a campaign of action, I would rate its effectiveness at about ten per cent."

"I don't comprehend—" Millbank began.

"In the first place, the moon faces the Graveyard only half of each month. In the second place, we have no reason to believe that the Basilisk will restrict himself to the Graveyard; if he has any intelligence, he will vary his field of attack. And thirdly, although perhaps of minor consequence, it would involve devoting the full use of our telescope to following ships across space, just at a time when we are in the middle of a very urgent agenda."

Dr. Murdock laughed at the expression on the faces of the insurance agents. "Professor Dexter loves the telescope more than his wife."

"If I had a wife," remarked Professor Dexter dryly.

There was silence, during which the steward began to serve dinner.

"Well, enough of the Basilisk for a while," said Dr. Murdock. "We're celebrating the sundown, and I think Doc Mole has honored us with fried chicken, mashed potatoes and country gravy."

Over coffee Commander Franchetti turned to Dick. "Won't it be lonely out here with no one your own age to pal around with?"

Dick considered. "I hardly think so. Not if the excitement keeps up."

"I suppose you're planning to be an astronomer like your father?"

Dick laughed. "Everybody asks me that. I don't know. I'm very much interested in stars and planets, but I think I'd rather visit them than look at them."

"Well, Dick," said Dr. Murdock, "I suppose you could stock up Crazy Sam's old raft with razor blades and snake oil and patent potato peelers and make a living as a trader."

"There's always the Space Navy," said Franchetti. "Although right now we have twenty thousand applications for every vacancy."

"I think I'd like the Space Navy," said Dick. He looked at Commander Franchetti. "Do you think —"

Franchetti laughed, shook his head. "Afraid not, Dick. See me in five years."

Professor Dexter said, "Dick could always become a pirate. It seems profitable enough. And, so far, safe."

Franchetti laughed again, a little painfully. "We're hoping it won't be safe long."

"I've been wondering about something," Dick said.

"And what's that?"

"Where did the Basilisk get his first ship?"

Franchetti shrugged. "I've no idea; I wish I did. The first we heard of the Basilisk was when the *Canopus* failed to make port. The Basilisk probably had men planted among the passengers."

"And then?"

"And then he apparently mounted guns aboard and runs it now as his flagship. That's my assumption."

Dr. Murdock had been toying with his spoon, listening absently. He said slowly, "We were comparing the Basilisk to the old pirates, comparing space to the Spanish Main. It's a good parallel. But where the old pirates had the Caribbean Islands for bases, the Basilisk is rather more restricted."

Franchetti scratched his cheek. "Well — to some extent. There's Venus, Earth, the Moon and Mars. Even on Earth he could find isolated regions where he could hide."

Professor Dexter said, "There's also the dark side of Mercury, the asteroids, and the satellites of Jupiter. Rather far out, but if the Basilisk operated on even a one-gravity acceleration, he could reach any point in the Solar System inside of four or five days."

"Need a lot of plutonium," Franchetti said doubtfully. "Plutonium is expensive. My guess is for somewhere close in."

"Perhaps his motivations are not entirely directed to profit. Although," Dexter continued, "I'm sure I can't imagine what they might be."

Dr. Murdock said, "It's rather suggestive that the attacks have all occurred in the Graveyard."

"Suggestive of what?"

"If his base were Mercury, we would expect to find the attacks closer to Venus or even Mars, since Mercury is on the same side of the sun. But the Graveyard is fairly close in to Earth and the moon."

"Naturally we've considered the moon," said Franchetti, "but compared with Venus, Mars or even Earth, it suffers disadvantages. It has no atmosphere, and any construction would be noticed almost at once."

"There are caves," said Dr. Murdock.

Professor Dexter said, "If you want to know anything about the moon, there's one man to ask: that's Sam Baxter. They call him Crazy Sam, but if there were a secret pirate base anywhere on the moon, he'd know it."

"He might even be the Basilisk himself," Dr. Murdock said with a laugh. "But I'll call old Sam in; there's no harm checking."

Crazy Sam was summoned, and a few moments later suspiciously pushed his head around the corner of the lounge. "Well, what do you want with me?"

"Sit down, Sam," said Dr. Murdock. "Have a cup of coffee. This is Commander Franchetti, who wants to ask you some questions."

Crazy Sam seated himself on the edge of a chair, where he poised as if prepared to jump up at any minute. "Ask ahead then, but if it's about gold or diamonds or moon-rubies, you can hold your tongue because I won't say a word. There's enough of such claptrap on Earth without adding more."

"No, no," said Dr. Murdock hastily. "Commander Franchetti is interested in hunting down pirates. He had an idea that they might be based somewhere on the moon."

Crazy Sam turned his pale gray glance on Franchetti. "Well, Commander, you can rest your mind. I know the moon like I know my hand. You could take me blindfolded anywhere, drop me in a crater and when I looked around, I'd tell you where I was. So — make yourself clear. Outside of us here at the observatory, there's nothing alive on the moon except a few of the natives, and they ain't pirates."

"Natives?"

"Yep. Natives. They live way down deep in the caves and never come up unless it's dark, and then they're scary as rabbits. They have big golden eyes the size of oranges and wear funny hats. I'm in pretty good with them; I've talked with 'em and they told me, 'Sam, you mind your business and we'll mind ours and we'll get along good together. But don't go mining any of them trashy jewels — ' "

Behind Sam's back Dexter shook his head significantly.

"Well, that's enough of that, Sam," said Dr. Murdock. "Just as long as the natives aren't pirates."

"Pirates — pooh!" He spat the word, then turning suddenly pushed his face to within six inches of Dick's. "And what do you think about it, boy?"

Dick said a little uneasily, "Well, I've heard you say there are natives and I've heard a few other people say there aren't. I'd like to see for myself."

Crazy Sam thumped him on the back. "Now that's sensible talk." He glanced at Dexter. "A lot more sensible than I get from some of you high-brows. Well," he turned back to Dick, "tomorrow you and I will go out for a ride and maybe we'll do a little prospecting."

"Will we see any of the natives?" Dick asked with mingled doubt and interest.

Crazy Sam looked at him sidewise. "Maybe. More likely not. It's still something early for 'em to be wandering up." He rose to his feet, turned back to Dr. Murdock. "If that's all, I'll be off to my kip."

He departed. Franchetti heaved a deep, humorous sigh. "He's emphatic enough."

"He's not quite as daffy as he sounds," said Dr. Murdock. "And he's honest. If there were any pirates here, he'd know and he'd tell you."

"And his talk about natives: what do you make of it?"

Dr. Murdock grinned. "I'm afraid I haven't seen any. I half suspect that Sam has bad dreams. But I could never go on the witness stand one way or the other." He looked at Dick. "Sam seems to have taken a fancy to you. Lots of men would give their eyeteeth to go prospecting with

Sam. He knows the first name of every crystal from here to Copernicus and back by the long way."

"Make him show you a few natives," said Commander Franchetti. "Better yet, bring a couple back with you."

# CHAPTER VI

## *Moon Treasure*

BY THE CLOCK IT WAS MORNING; the sun, however, was nowhere to be seen, and the light that shone upon the observatory came from the half-globe of Earth. Concrete glowed with the soft luster of a pearl, the lava glass of the crater floor spread out like a dark lake. The big telescope, a gaunt shape on the crater wall, stood like an unfriendly sentry, seemingly magnified by a trick of Earthlight to dimensions twice its normal size.

Dick, waiting while Crazy Sam loaded extra fuel aboard his raft, shivered inside his space-suit.

Crazy Sam rapped on Dick's helmet. Dick jumped around startled. "Look sharp now, boy," snapped Sam.

"Well, yes," said Dick puzzled. "But just what do you want me to do?"

"Jump aboard, we're ready to scoot. You sit on the bench here and hang on, because ol' Bronco Bert takes the bit in his teeth."

Dick climbed aboard; Crazy Sam took a wide look around the sky, like a farmer consulting the weather, then followed suit.

Dr. Murdock, standing by the window, waved; Dick waved in return. The raft lurched, rose at a violent slant. Dick hung on for dear life.

"Move to the right, boy," cried Crazy Sam. "Two inches — we've got to balance." He eased open a valve. "This isn't one of them trans-space liners with gyros to do all your thinking for you. Ol' Bert here, you got to whip him into line. Ho now, Bert, behave yourself."

Crazy Sam worked at his controls and Dick watched with interest. They were simple and forthright: a mixer gauge, a master feed valve, small bar valves controlling each of the four jets, and a joy stick.

"Balance, balance," muttered Crazy Sam, touching first one and then another of the valve handles. "Every time I go up, it's different." He barked suddenly, "No wriggling there, boy! Whenever you give a jump, then I got to twist these valves."

Dick sat like a statue, and the raft skittered over the lunar landscape. It was like riding a poorly designed rowboat; there was the same feeling of delicate pressures and vague instability. Easing his head to the side and looking over Sam's shoulder, Dick finally understood the controls. Pushing the joy stick forward turned the jets aft, providing forward thrust. Then, to compensate for the loss of support, Sam was obliged to ease open the master valve, so that the first few moments of flight were a series of rather alarming swoops, dips and accelerations.

At last Crazy Sam got his fractious craft into balance, and they skimmed swiftly over the lava flows of the lunar sea.

The speaker crackled in Dick's ear, and Crazy Sam's voice was almost jovial, "Well, boy, what's it look like to you?"

Dick surveyed the lava flow, a sea of crusty black rock with fringes of silver Earthlight, like white lace on a million black petticoats. "I'd hate to walk home."

"Yep," chuckled Crazy Sam, "you'd be a long time. See that opening down there?" They rode over a crevasse two hundred feet wide, stretching straight as a beam of black light across the lunar sea. "Well, that's Baxter Gap. That's what I calls it anyway. It's a thousand feet deep, and there's some strange sights down at the bottom, which maybe you wouldn't believe if I told you — so I won't."

"No, really," protested Dick, "I —"

Crazy Sam cut him short. "All in good time, boy. There's lots of moon to see and we'll take it easy, the simple things first. You wouldn't want to grow up to be like me, would you?"

Dick, unable to follow the sequence of thoughts, made polite but noncommittal sounds. Crazy Sam was not deceived. He laughed a short, sardonic cackle. "Well, I got this way — a little jumpy you might say — from prowling in and out of places nobody invited me into. And now it's got into my blood, and I couldn't leave if I wanted to — which I don't. Any day you name I could take a sack and in two hours I'd come back with emeralds like green coach lamps, sapphires and rubies big as cantaloupes — and pure!" Sam's voice became reverent. "Boy, until you've seen a moon-ruby glowing in the sun, you've never seen red!" He sighed. "But no, that's bad money. And my old bones couldn't stand up to Earth gravity any more."

He pointed ahead. "Now we're coming to Baxter Point, as I calls it. That big black peak. It's the tallest crag in this section of the moon. Down near the foot is a kind of grotto completely lined with needles of platinum so that it looks like a porcupine turned inside out. Baxter's Platinum Palace, I calls it," he added thoughtfully.

Dick looked around the horizon. To the right spread the tumbled black lava of the sea; to the left lay a series of small craters, and ahead rose Baxter Point. "Do we pass near the Security Station?"

"No," said Crazy Sam shortly.

"I'd like to go with you the next time you go out." He waited, but Crazy Sam made no reply. "You're caretaker, aren't you?"

"Yes," snapped Sam, "I'm caretaker, and I take care to keep my nose in joint."

Dick puzzled silently over the remark. Crazy Sam answered the unspoken question. "I mean that they never had any right blasting out hangars and digging into them old caves the way they did. They disturbed the natives; frightened them back into hiding, and they're just beginning to come back up again. They don't like to be bothered and I don't like to be bothered. I leave them alone and they leave me alone. Now that's enough; I ain't gonna show you no natives because you'd want to photograph them with that fancy gadget of yours, and show the pictures around, and the first thing you know there'd be committees and expeditions, with a thousand high-brows like Professor Dexter coming out to clutter up the moon, and I might as well just head old Bert here up into space and have done with the whole shebang…Well, that's enough. We're going over the Edge now."

"The Edge?"

"The Edge of the visible face of the moon. We're going to the side that's always hidden from Earth. Look there ahead, that's the Great Baxter Crater, biggest and steepest on the whole moon."

For a period they skidded on in silence, and presently the edge of the sun showed over the horizon, casting black shadows ten miles long. Below passed the black fantasies of the moon mountains, crags like rows of inverted icicles, gulfs like mirrors held to the black of space.

From time to time Crazy Sam bent his head to examine a fuel gauge; and at last he said, "We've gone through a third of our fuel, so we'd better think about stopping. Now let's see, where are we…" He glanced around the landscape. "Yep, there's Baxter Mesa yonder, and off in the distance is the Sam Baxter Range. Right down under the mesa is a likely piece of territory that I haven't looked at too close. Who knows? We might find something a little special." He manipulated valves and joy stick; the raft slowed, settled in a series of lurches and sudden sinkings.

Under the mesa was a ledge twenty feet wide, bounded by a crack like a black wound into the moon. Dick gripped the edge of the raft in excitement and alarm; Crazy Sam was evidently planning to land on the ledge. If he miscalculated, if the jets sputtered and the raft made a freakish sidestep, they might strike against the edge of the abyss, overturn, and fall into unknowable depths.

The raft grounded, four feet in from the edge of the emptiness. Dick sat for a minute, letting his heart settle back into place. He relaxed his grip, and inside the gauntlets his fingers were cramped.

Crazy Sam, who had hopped spryly to the ground, turned his head, called out testily, "Well, boy, are you coming?"

Dick stepped off the raft, peered cautiously over the lip of the precipice. "I wouldn't care to fall into Baxter's Bottomless Pit."

Crazy Sam looked at him suspiciously. "How'd you know the name of this place? Don't know as I've ever mentioned it."

"I just guessed," said Dick.

Crazy Sam snorted. "Well, get your pick and come along. I see a lode of nice-looking porphyry over here that I don't recollect having noticed before."

Dick looked dubiously along the ledge. The pinnacles of the Sam Baxter Range broke up the level glare of the sunlight; deceptive pools of black shadow lay along the ledge. He asked, "What is porphyry?"

Crazy Sam pointed to the sheer rock face, large dark crystals in a pale gray matrix. "When it's spotted with crystals like a leopard, then it's porphyry."

Dick looked closely at the rock face. "Are all those crystals valuable?"

"Nope. Just common old hornblende and mica, most of it. But once in a while..." He leaned forward suddenly like a hawk sighting a rabbit, hopped down the ledge, tapped with his pick. He broke off a chunk of rock, tapped a little more, very delicately, and held up a glistening object about an inch thick and six inches long. "Once in a while you get something like this."

Dick took the crystal, a six-sided pencil, like ice frozen in layers of different colors: rose-red, yellow, water-clear, green. "What on earth is this?"

Crazy Sam chuckled. "On Earth it's called tourmaline. I guess there's no harm calling it tourmaline out here too. That's a small one. I've knocked out crystals as long as my arm with all the colors of the rainbow."

Dick turned to the porphyry with new interest and pounded the rock wall as he had seen Crazy Sam do.

"No, no," said Sam peevishly. "Don't try to knock a hole in the hill; tap it gentle-like on the cleavage lines. Rock is just like wood — it splits easy some directions, hard in others."

Dick walked along the porphyry face, rapping, tapping, and presently was rewarded with three or four crystals, one even larger than the one Sam had found.

A stratum of dense black stone angled down across the porphyry. At the plane of intersection he noticed that the porphyry seemed stained, soft, almost like old putty. With the sharp end of his pick he pried at a chunk of the metamorphosed porphyry. It came loose, dropped down to the ledge, slow as a balloon under the weak lunar gravity. Dick started to turn back toward the raft, but first gave the chunk a rap for luck. It broke open like an egg. Colored fire, a flash of pure purple, caught Dick's eye. Slowly, in wonder and awe, he bent over, picked up the jewel; a perfect, many-sided crystal, twice as large as his thumb nail and glowing with purple as rich and intense as Tyrian dye.

He ran back through pools of alternate shadow and glare toward the raft. Crazy Sam was nowhere in sight.

He hesitated, looking up and down the ledge, anxious to show Sam his find, eager also to return to the vein of soft rock. But Sam had vanished around the bend in the ledge. Dick started to put the purple jewel in his pouch, but feeling the tourmaline crystals, hesitated. His eye fell on Sam's toolbox, a handy place to keep his finds until they returned to the observatory. He lifted the lid. The box was almost empty, containing a few wrenches, and a notebook carelessly thrown on top, and lying open. Dick started to place his tourmalines on the paper when the superscription caught his eye. It read, "Chart and Directions, the Baxter Caves, for private use only."

Dick's lump of curiosity throbbed like a boil. He bent his head over the page. A series of rectangles were arranged in the shape of an L. Superimposed was a pattern of red and blue lines, apparently drawn with crayon pencil.

There was vibration behind him; a hand reached in front of him, slammed down the lid of the toolbox. Dick turned to look into Crazy Sam's furious face.

"Nosy kid, just like the rest of 'em," snarled Sam. "Can't trust you out of my sight without you snoopin' and pryin' and —"

"I wasn't either," cried Dick. "I opened the box to —"

"Never mind," roared Sam. "It makes no difference. Get aboard the raft; we're going back to the observatory, and that'll be all of that!"

Dick sullenly took his seat on the bench. Sam had taken it for granted that Dick was spying; there was nothing more Dick's pride would allow him to say. He thrust the purple jewel into his pouch, held on to the bench.

The jets spewed silent blue flame, the raft rose from the ledge, slewed alarmingly into the chasm, and Dick's heart leaped up into his throat.

Sam twirled the master valve, pulled back the joy stick and the raft climbed up over Baxter Mesa.

Halfway back to the observatory, Sam, looking straight ahead, said abruptly, "Maybe you have noticed a piece of scribblin' in the toolbox."

"Yes," said Dick shortly. "I saw a piece of paper."

"Well," said Sam, "it was just a silly idea of mine. Don't mean a thing in the world, you understand? Nothing whatever." He paused, but Dick made no reply.

"Well," asked Sam anxiously. "Did you hear me?"

"Yes, I heard you."

"But you don't say nothing."

Dick shrugged. "There's nothing to say. You accused me of spying, then next you say there was nothing to see."

"That's right, nothing whatever. Just the same," and Sam's voice took on a deeper, harder note, "it don't pay to be too snoopy, too inquisitive, around the moon. Get me?" He turned his head around an alarming distance, like a parrot.

Dick looked for long seconds into the pinched, sand-colored face. Behind the pale gray eyes he seemed to sense a phosphorescent flurry of tiny electric sparks. A shiver of uneasiness ran up his spine, like ice water filling a tube.

Sam asked in a menacing voice, "Understand me, boy?"

"Yes," said Dick. "I understand what you're saying." And he said to himself, but that doesn't mean I'll pay any attention.

# CHAPTER VII

## The Perfect Crime

DR. MURDOCK CAME INTO the lounge, tossed the woolen gloves which he had worn under the space-suit gauntlets into a cupboard. Looking around, he saw Dick sitting quietly by a window. He crossed the room, pulled up a chair. "I didn't expect you back so soon."

Dick said a little uncomfortably, "It was Sam's idea, not mine."

Dr. Murdock cocked his head to the side, considered Dick from the corner of his eye. "How did you and Sam get along?"

Dick shrugged. "Very well, for the most part." He paused. Dr. Murdock waited patiently, knowing from long experience that Dick would presently get around to the story.

Dick reached in his pocket. "We saw a lot of country," he said, "most of it named after Sam."

Dr. Murdock laughed. "I've heard about Sam's self-immortalizing tendencies. And did you find anything?"

Dick handed him the purple crystal. Dr. Murdock leaned forward, whistled. "What in the world is this?"

"I don't know."

"I've never seen anything like it. Didn't Sam know?"

"Sam hasn't seen it." Dick described how he had found the jewel, and the toolbox incident. "So I never had a chance to show him the crystal — whatever it is."

"Rubies are red, sapphires blue, emeralds green," Dr. Murdock mused, "but except for amethysts, which are very pale, I know of no purple stones. Certainly nothing as fiery and rich as this." He rubbed it on his sleeve. "Next week I've got to hop over to Earth for a few days. I can't take you with me this time, but I'll take the jewel and have it valued. It might be a unique stone, and if it is, you'll have a very nice bank account."

"If it's really valuable," said Dick with enthusiasm, "maybe we could get some more. I'm sure I could find that ledge."

"Well, you wait till I get back from Earth. Then maybe we'll run out to Baxter's Bottomless Pit again."

Dick looked up through the window to the great half-globe of Earth. "When are you leaving?" he asked rather wistfully.

"In about a week. A radiogram came this morning from the Board of Trustees. I'll be very rushed and very busy, otherwise I'd want you to come along. I'll catch the *Australian Star* coming in from Venus."

"If it gets here," said Dick gloomily.

Dr. Murdock looked surprised and thoughtful. After a moment he said, "I'd almost forgotten the Basilisk. It seems like a bad dream. But I think the *Australian Star* will arrive safely enough. All ships — according to Commander Franchetti — have been ordered to keep radio silence from the time they leave port and take courses away from the normal lanes."

"I'd like to go with you," said Dick.

Dr. Murdock laughed. "Next time, and then we'll spend a month. Don't worry, Earth will be there a long while. And now I'm going up to relieve Professor Dexter at the Eye. We're making a new set of plates for the Corvus region." He rose to his feet. "Like to come along? If you want to be an astronomer, you'll have to learn how to use a telescope."

Dick arose; they went into the dressing room, climbed into space-suits and set out across the floor of the crater.

The next week passed uneventfully and, for Dick, very swiftly. He explored the walls of the crater near the observatory, carrying a geologist's hammer. He tapped and hammered at formations which looked promising, but found nothing more exciting than big gleaming cubes of pyrite.

Part of each day he spent at the telescope, and an hour or so in the library. The great bulk of material on file was photographic plates:

hundreds of thousands of black squares, each specked with stars. Recreational reading for observatory personnel was stocked only as an afterthought. Here also was the ten-volume *New Universal Star Index*, to which Librarian Isel Bayer had devoted twelve years of his life and which, so he informed Dick, was by no means completed. "Every time a new plate leaves Dexter's darkroom, it means another three days' work for me. Look." He went to his desk and picked up two plates, which he gave to Dick. "These are the same section of sky, on the same scale. Do you see any difference?"

Dick studied the plates. "This one marked AX has a lot more stars on it."

Isel Bayer nodded and his fluffy white hair waved like ostrich plumes. Even in the subdued light of the library he wore his dark glasses. "That's one of the new Corvus plates. This other one was photographed by the Harvard Camera, a hundred-inch reflector on the Harvard University's artificial satellite. Naturally our telescope, collecting over ten times as much light, records many more stars. My job is to find and index them with their exact positions."

Dick compared the two plates, glancing from one to the other. "This AX photo is photographed in color; I can see reds and blues and greens."

"Very pale of course," said Isel Bayer. He had a baritone voice, extraordinarily rich and resonant, and rather incongruous in his spindly body. "In any event, we soon discovered the old indexes to be inadequate; and I have based this new index on an entirely new and rational principle."

For the next half-hour he explained the system to the fidgeting Dick, who was not particularly interested. But Isel Bayer's voice never halted, rising and falling dramatically like a singer's. At last Dick, after looking at his watch, jumped to his feet. "I've got to meet my father; we're going up to the telescope."

Behind the dark glasses Isel Bayer's eyes seemed to flash, with what might have been amusement or irritation. Dick cared little, one way or the other; he found that he did not especially like Isel Bayer. His jackstraw frame, the cloud of silver hair, and the droning conversation were facets of the scholarly librarian. But the dark glasses seemed to mask a second personality, more in accordance with a certain spidery muscularity Dick noticed in the long white fingers.

Dick ran down to the lounge where he found Hutchings, the young bookkeeper. "If you're looking for your father," said Hutchings sourly, "he's already gone out, just this minute. He wants you to come right along."

"Thanks." Dick hastened into his space-suit, sealed the dome over his head, and plugged a new tank of oxygen into place. He went into the exit chamber, closed the door, started the pump which exhausted the air. A moment later the outer door swung open automatically and Dick stepped out on the crater floor.

He paused for a moment; no matter how many times he left the shelter of the building, he had never become accustomed to the sudden feeling of nakedness before the stars. On Venus the perpetual overcast allowed no intimation of space. Here the moon seemed to hold him up as if on a plate for the scrutiny of the heavens. And the face of space seemed harder, more brilliant and powerful even than the face of the moon.

Dick shook off the feeling, ran around the administration building with the long bounds which weak lunar gravity made possible.

He saw his father standing perfectly still near the crater wall. Dick hesitated in his stride, came to a stop. There was something peculiar in his father's attitude, something strained and tense.

Dick ran forward. Dr. Murdock turned his head, saw him coming, but made no move. Dick came up beside him. "What's the matter?"

Dr. Murdock made no immediate answer; in sudden alarm Dick peered through the dome up into his father's face.

"I'm all right," said Dr. Murdock in a tight voice. "There's nothing wrong. It's just what might have happened if I hadn't turned around to see if you were coming."

Dick looked around the crater. So far as he could see, there was nothing alarming in sight. "But what happened?"

Dr. Murdock glanced up toward the sky. "As near as I can make out, a meteor missed my head by about two inches." He nodded toward a chunk of gray rock resting a few feet distant on the crater floor. "If I hadn't just happened to look around…" His voice trailed off.

Dick looked anxiously around the sky, around the crater walls, then back to the chunk of rock. "It couldn't have been coming very fast or it would have splintered."

"Fast enough to have caved in my helmet."

"But meteors usually travel at several miles a second," Dick protested.

"I'm not concerned how fast the thing was going," snapped Dr. Murdock. "I'm only glad that it missed me." He blew out his breath. "Phew...One chance in a hundred million and I happened to walk into it." He gave his head a quick nervous shake. "That was a close shave."

"It seems very strange," said Dick.

His father looked at him oddly. "How do you mean 'strange'?"

"Well—if anyone wanted to kill you and escape without suspicion, he couldn't pick a better way than to brain you with a fake meteor."

Dr. Murdock laughed uncertainly. "I'm afraid you've got murder on the brain. Why should anyone want to kill me?"

"No one had any reason to kill Dr. Vrosnek, but he died in a freak accident."

Dr. Murdock was suddenly silent. Dick went to look at the meteor. "This can't be where it struck?"

"No." Dr. Murdock pointed. "It hit along in there and bounced."

Dick bent over the glass. "Which mark?"

"Which mark?" repeated his father in puzzlement.

"There're three marks about six inches apart—and the rock is only four inches in diameter."

Together they examined the marks—crushed white spots with lines radiating out star-fashion. Dr. Murdock rose slowly to his feet. "It does seem peculiar," he said uncertainly. "One meteor could not make three marks. I suppose one is not inconceivable—a freak accident certainly, if it had hit me. Two in the same place is rather rich. And three!" He turned, scanned the crater wall as Dick had done.

Dick asked suddenly, "Where were you standing when the rock came down?"

"Why—right about here." Dr. Murdock moved a step. "It came close enough to tick against my helmet."

Dick bent close over the mark, sighted up past his father's head.

"From here, it looks as if it came from the crater wall, just to the right of that tall white bluff." He pointed to a knob of rock a hundred yards distant.

His father said reflectively: "Suppose, for the sake of argument, someone did have it in for me. How could he be sure of hitting me at such a distance? He could certainly get the rock here in this weak gravity, but a man couldn't throw with enough force to do much more than dent a helmet — even if he were able to hit me at a hundred yards."

Dick pointed to the marks. "Somehow he was able to get his rocks down here to hit not more than a foot apart."

"It sounds like some sort of catapult." Dr. Murdock looked at the white bluff.

Dick said, "I'll run up and take a look." He started forward.

"No…You'd better stay here. If someone were up there, he would have seen us and taken his catapult and himself away by this time."

Dick reluctantly returned. "Someone here on the moon is very clever." And he glanced up along the crater wall. "If that rock had hit you, it would have been a perfect crime."

His father said in a distant voice, "I suppose you're right. 'Regrettable accident takes Dr. Paul Murdock.' It seems so completely unreal."

"Pirates are unreal too."

"But why should pirates want to kill me? What good would it do? None whatever."

"Perhaps they hope to install one of their own men as the next Chief Astronomer."

Dr. Murdock shook his head. "Impossible. Dexter's next in line, then Isel Bayer. I can't imagine two less likely pirates than either Dexter or Bayer."

Dick, remembering Bayer's dark glasses, was not so sure. And yet, had he not just left Bayer in the library? Could he have possibly climbed into a space-suit, run around the observatory, climbed the crater wall, and somehow propelled a stone at Dr. Murdock, all before Dick had left the building? In Dick's mind's eye appeared a sudden image of Isel Bayer's long heron-legs scissoring rapidly across the crater; the picture was so incongruous that he almost laughed.

Dr. Murdock said in a subdued voice, "I suppose we'd better say nothing of this. If someone is actually out to get me — it seems fantastic even to say it — he knows he has failed. If it was an accident —" the idea seemed to hearten him "— as it probably was, we'll serve no purpose raising a furore."

They climbed slowly toward the telescope. Halfway up the hill Dick said, "If the same person who tried to kill you murdered Dr. Vrosnek, how would he have gone about it?"

"Killing Dr. Vrosnek, you mean?"

"Yes. How could he have killed Dr. Vrosnek?"

Dr. Murdock had regained most of his composure, and with it his first skepticism. "In the first place, Dick, we haven't proved a thing one way or the other."

"How do you account for the three marks, and for the fact that the meteor came from the crater wall? And also that it didn't smash to pieces when it struck?"

"A meteor might come from any direction and at almost any speed. And as for the marks, I really have no idea."

"Well," said Dick desperately, "just suppose that someone purposely killed Dr. Vrosnek, how would he do it?"

Dr. Murdock shuddered. "I can't believe that anyone would perform such a fiendish act."

"But just suppose someone did!"

Dr. Murdock reluctantly turned the idea over in his mind. "First the murderer would have to swing the tube to the sun; then drop the shield."

"Wouldn't Dr. Vrosnek have noticed the motion of the tube?"

"No, not if he were making a time exposure. After he started the celestial drive he might easily get busy with paperwork. The next thing he would know, there would be a flood of fire, and a moment later —" He shook his head. "But I still don't think it's reasonable. For this reason. There are two sets of controls, one in the cage and one in the lower office. But when the cage controls are in use, the office controls are automatically cut out of the circuit."

"How about the sun-shield?"

"Well, I suppose the system could be disrupted easily enough from the office, but it would do no harm unless the tube were pointing directly at the sun."

"Was Dr. Vrosnek working on a part of the sky close to the sun when he was killed?"

Dr. Murdock stopped beside the lower office, looked quizzically at Dick. "I think you're growing up to be more of a detective than an astronomer…I don't know about Dr. Vrosnek. No one ever said anything about it."

"Let's look at the office controls."

Dr. Murdock shrugged. "It can't do any harm."

They entered the inner office by an air lock, unsealed and hinged back their helmets. Dr. Murdock went to a panel in the wall, opened it to display a row of dials and switches. He pointed here and there. "This is the right-ascension setting, this the declination. You set these and servo-motors automatically swing the telescope to the set position. Then this switch here controls the celestial motion. But when the controls in the cage are in use, a contact, behind this piece of plastic here, opens."

Dick looked intently at the heads of the machine screws. His father watched with a trace of amusement. "What do you see?"

"It looks a little scratched. Is there a screwdriver anywhere around?"

Dr. Murdock opened a drawer, handed him one, still with an air of mild, indulgent amusement.

Dick unscrewed the panel. "Are those the contacts there?"

"That's right."

"Then if someone pushed them together, or shorted across them, he could use the controls down here."

"Correct."

Dick squinted, peered. "Look at the face of the contacts."

Dr. Murdock, suddenly interested, peered at the copper faces. "Scratched." He rubbed his chin.

"As if something had been wedged in between, like a knife blade, or a file, or a screwdriver."

Dr. Murdock made a dubious sound. "Well, it's possible, but again there's nothing definite. Still, there's no point in being reckless. When I reach Earth I'll get in touch with the UN Bureau of Investigation and ask for a special investigator. In the meantime," he looked anxiously at

Dick, "you must be very careful. And don't do any more detecting. If these —" he hesitated "— accidents are more than mere accidents, and whoever is responsible decided that you were troublesome, you might find yourself in considerable danger."

# CHAPTER VIII

## The Coded Message

DICK WATCHED THE DISPATCH BOAT, piloted by A. B. Sende, dwindle to a dot over the dark lunar sea, the blue down-jets trailing like legs on a flea. If Sende were the criminal, thought Dick anxiously, he could easily find some means of murdering his father while they waited for the *Australian Star*. But if Sende were the murderer, how had he managed to kill Dr. Vrosnek when he had arrived on the moon only a short time before?

Dick's thoughts drifted to Isel Bayer; it suddenly occurred to him that in some peculiar manner Bayer and Sende resembled each other. He could not put his finger on the characteristic they shared; possibly something in their posture or the way they held their heads, or even the slenderness common to both. Remembering Sende's quince-yellow eyes, Dick idly wondered what lay behind Isel Bayer's dark glasses. He looked around, but Dexter and Bayer, who had both come to see Dr. Murdock off, had gone inside the administration building.

The dispatch boat was gone. A hundred miles above the moon it would take up an orbit, coasting at a speed just sufficient to counter the gravity of the moon. Then presently the *Australian Star* would drift down from the black space ocean, radio contact would be made, the boat and ship would come together.

Dick started back to the administration building, feeling lonesome and somewhat at a loss. He moved slowly, having no desire for conversation or company. He stopped short, looked across the crater toward the telescope. Almost by their own volition, his legs took him to where his father had escaped the pseudo-meteor. He bent curiously over the spot where the stone had struck, but to his astonishment the marks had disappeared.

Dick rose to his feet, looked around the crater. Beyond question this was where his father had stood; he had marked it by a pair of converging ripples in the black glass. But where were the star-shaped cracks in the glass?

There was a prickling at the back of his neck, as if eyes were fixed on him. He took a quick look toward the administration building; something flickered at one of the windows. A face?

Uneasily he returned to the inspection of the black glass. A rough depression in the obsidian caught his eye, near where he remembered the three marks. Had someone come out and chipped away the evidence? He drew back suddenly, thinking that if his father's enemy were standing at the catapult now, his head was dead on target. But looking up at the bluff of white feldspar, he decided that nerves were stampeding his imagination. Whatever contrivance had launched the rock, it must have been dismantled long ago.

Once again Dick looked across to the buildings of the observatory. They shone in the soft white light of Earth, now at full. The floor of the crater spread out behind, quiet as a dark mirror, stretching ten miles to the opposite wall.

No one was in sight; at this particular moment no one would be at the telescope. Dick checked his oxygen tank: plenty for another four hours.

Hoping that no one was following his movements, he ran quickly for the white bluff, moving in twenty- and thirty-foot bounds. He sprang up the cliff, jumping from foothold to foothold like a mountain goat. A few moments later he stood on the round crest of the bluff. Carefully he looked around the landscape, but so far as he could see, no one had noticed his movements.

He moved back a little, surveyed the surface of the bluff and the crater wall behind. It was a wild patchwork of silver, black, gray — crazy-angled shapes, planes, edges, like a very bad abstract painting. It required a real effort to bring the tangle of forms into perspective. He noticed a set of razor-edged ridges slanting down from the main wall to form three dark little valleys, all more or less shaded from the Earthlight. Dick checked the spot on the crater floor where the rock had struck, turned back to the dark little pockets. From the first of these, a man could well have rigged his catapult, fired a pair of test shots to check the accuracy of his aim, then waited until Dr. Murdock crossed the line of fire — all completely unseen.

Dick cautiously stepped forward into the gulch. For a moment he could see nothing; then his eyes became accustomed to the reflected Earthlight, which seeped in to outline vaguely a few boulders and ridges.

He looked around uneasily. If traces of the catapult still remained in the dark hollow, he would be unable to see them without a light. A new thought came to freeze him in his tracks: not impossibly, some devilish arrangement might be waiting — a deadfall, land mine, a gun trap. Dick started gingerly back out of the hollow, the sense of danger almost strong enough to taste.

On the great luminous disk of Earth a black silhouette appeared. Dick's heart stood still.

The shape paused, the head twisted, peered into the valley. Dick, sweating clammily inside his suit, reached to the ground, picked up a rock. The movement attracted the attention of the newcomer, the head inside the helmet twisted sharply. The speaker inside Dick's helmet hummed. "Is that you in there, Dick?"

Dick recognized the voice — Hutchings, the pinch-faced young bookkeeper. He took a deep breath. "Yes, it's me."

"What are you doing up here sneaking around these rocks?"

Dick came forward. "What business is it of yours?"

Hutchings sniffed. "Your father made it my business. He told me to keep an eye on you, not to let you go off too far by yourself; although what difference it makes, I don't know."

"Well, you can forget it. I don't need you trailing around behind me."

"I've got orders." The orders had been a few hasty words over Dr. Murdock's shoulder; Hutchings had received them sullenly; but now, observing Dick's resentment, a new vista of entertainment opened before his eyes. By obeying Dr. Murdock's orders to the letter, he could indulge himself in a good deal of subtle bullying, at the same time presenting an air of righteousness to anyone who called him to account.

Hutchings had a thin monkey-face with black eyebrows and a perpetually sour mouth. He had obtained his job because of a distant relationship with the late Dr. Vrosnek. He had come out to the moon expecting to scoop up diamonds and moon-rubies by the bucketful. A few halfhearted prospecting trips had shown him nothing but black rock and gloomy shadows. Observatory routine bored him, and the project of tormenting Dick came like a draught of cool water to a thirsty man.

"Yep," Hutchings said, gloating at the sight of Dick's angry face, "your father told me to keep an eye on you, see that you didn't get lost or wander too far away from the observatory. And that's what I'm going to do."

Dick's fury allowed him no words; he turned and marched back down the hill. Now he thought of a ruse to annoy Hutchings. If Hutchings planned to keep an eye on him, he'd have to work at the job. Dick gave a sudden spring which carried him thirty feet up the slope. Another, and another. He dodged behind a jut of black rock, dived to the side, doubled back, scrambled up a slope of broken rock, and came out on top of a sawtoothed ridge.

Hutchings was nowhere in sight, but his voice came to Dick's ears by the radio: a stream of angry calls and muttered threats. Dick laughed contentedly. A new idea occurred to him. He scanned the crater wall; then, climbing a series of ledges, came out on the skyline. He called into the microphone, "Where are you, Hutchings? I thought you were planning to keep an eye on me."

Hutchings appeared two hundred yards below, looking angrily around the rocks.

"I'm up here," called Dick, "and I'm going down the other side. If you're going to keep an eye on me, you'll have to move a little faster."

"When I catch up with you, you sneaky little blatherskite, you'll wish you'd stayed on Venus where you belong!" Hutchings started furiously up the hill.

Dick dropped over the ridge, ran a hundred yards along a convenient ledge, jumped up to the ridge, looked down along the crater wall.

Hutchings was visible, clambering up the slope, progressing by ungainly, floundering leaps. Dick chuckled, now enjoying Hutchings' crusade. Hutchings heard the chuckle and shouted, "I'll beat your ears in when I catch you!"

Dick carefully slipped down into the shadow of a tall spire of rock, and as Hutchings disappeared over the ridge, he dropped down the crater wall as fast as he could, reached the glass, and ran with fifty-foot bounds toward the observatory. He reached the administration building and ducked into the lock chamber.

Hutchings, nowhere in sight, presumably was searching for him, shouting threats on the far side of the crater wall.

With great satisfaction Dick removed his space-suit, hung it in the locker, and went up to his room to take a shower and change his clothes.

Two hours later Hutchings returned. Dick was sitting alone in the lounge reading. Hutchings stormed in, his face white with rage; without a word he started across the lounge.

Dick jumped to his feet, drew back the book to throw it. Hutchings was undersized but wiry, and more than a match for Dick in a fight. Dick knew that he must use his wits as well as his strength if he wished to escape a beating.

He sidled behind a chair. "Come out from behind there, you miserable little coward," Hutchings panted.

For an answer, Dick hit him over the head with the book.

Hutchings roared, lifted up the chair, flung it at Dick. Dick stumbled, fell; Hutchings was on him, kicking viciously. Pain shot through Dick's ribs. He rolled, grabbed one of Hutchings' feet just as the other caught him in the cheek. Stars blinded him, his teeth creaked; he pulled at the foot. Hutchings tottered, and beating the air, fell over backward. Dick dived at him, striking out with both fists. He hit a chin and an eye. Hutchings bellowed.

"Here, here," said an angry voice. "What's going on!" Professor Dexter strode between them.

Hutchings' manner underwent an instant change. "I'm just protecting myself, Doctor; just because he's the Chief Astronomer's son, he thinks he can get away with murder!"

"Nothing of the sort," cried Dick.

Breathlessly, Hutchings went on. "Dr. Murdock asked me to keep an eye on him, to see that he didn't get into trouble. I was obeying my instructions, but Dick didn't like it, and as soon as I got back in the building he threw this book at me."

"That's not true," Dick protested vehemently. "He came at me himself; he was angry because I ducked him and came back in."

Professor Dexter allowed a rather annoyed smile to cross his face. "Whatever the cause of the trouble, I want no more of it. Do you hear, both of you?"

"The less I see of him the better," growled Dick.

"I'm supposed to watch him," said Hutchings maliciously.

Professor Dexter inspected him with distaste. "And who does your work while you watch Dick?"

"I'm all caught up, and anyway I'm just obeying orders."

"My father never told him to trail me around like a dog," said Dick. "I know him better than that."

Professor Dexter said impatiently, "Well, he'll be back in a few days and then you can hash it all out one way or the other. Meantime, no more rows. Hutchings, you better go and attend to your eye."

After Hutchings had left, Professor Dexter turned to Dick. "I don't want to be arbitrary, Dick, but I think that until your father comes back you'd better not go out alone. Any number of things can happen to a person wandering around by himself: his oxygen tank can jar loose; he can get his foot caught in a crevice; he could even fall into one of the chasms. It's dangerous, and while I have no doubt that Hutchings is exceeding the scope of your father's instructions, in theory it's a good idea that nobody goes out alone on the moon."

Dick nodded. He was both angry and disappointed, but he could not challenge the justice of Professor Dexter's decision. "Just as you say." He picked up his book, set the chair on its feet, and wincing at the ache in his ribs, settled himself to his reading.

Dinner for Dick was rather uncomfortable, and probably even more so for Hutchings, who took considerable ribbing in regard to his black eye. Immediately afterward Dick went to his room, where for want of better occupation he began to tinker with his portable radio — a fruitless occupation, since there was only one broadcast frequency on the moon, the official observatory band reserved for news broadcasts and important communications. Consequently Dick, dialing down the wavelengths, was astonished to hear a voice coming from the loud-speaker reading off a list of numbers and letters.

He hurriedly checked the station selector, but found nothing wrong. Meanwhile the voice went on — a voice that Dick found both familiar and strange; try as he might, he was unable to identify it. On sudden impulse he seized pencil and paper and began to copy the numbers and letters as they were spoken: "RGA66953 CMP55248 TWZ72221 BJO48438..." The voice continued for three or four minutes, then cut off sharply.

Dick sat staring at the little set, the short hairs at the back of his neck prickling. There was something uncanny and frightening about this voice speaking where no voice should speak. Sende was radio opera-tor; was it Sende's voice? Dick could not be sure. However, to the best of his knowledge, here at the observatory was the only broadcasting station on the moon. Perhaps if he hurried down he might surprise the mysterious broadcaster in the act.

He ran out of the room, down the stairs, along the tube to the radio shack. The door was locked. He knocked on the door. No answer. He waited a moment or two, then doubtfully backed down the corridor.

Hard hands gripped his shoulders. Dick shuddered, froze stiff. Slowly he turned around, fearing what he might see.

Sende's glittering golden eyes looked into his from a distance of six inches; the hooked nose almost touched his. "Hello, young fellow," came Sende's hard, dry voice. "And what are you doing down here?"

Dick stared into the eyes; they seemed to grow larger, to stare ter-ribly into his. He blinked; they were yellow eyes of normal size. "I...I came down to see if you had come back," he said haltingly. "I was won-dering if my father had gotten away all right."

Sende made no answer. Dick backed away from him, turned and ran down the corridor. He climbed the stairs, pounded on Professor Dexter's door.

"Come in," came Dexter's sharp voice. Dick burst into the room. "Well, Dick?"

Dexter was seated at his desk, wearing a black satin bathrobe; with his black hair, black eyes, and stern white face he looked like a particularly intelligent Roman senator.

"Well, Dick?" said Dexter once more.

Without any preliminaries Dick burst into his story. "I just happened to hear a voice reading these numbers. I thought it was strange — something to do with the pirates — so I ran down to the radio shack. It was locked, but right outside I met Sende. I'm not sure, but it sounded something like his voice. A little deeper and fuller, perhaps."

Professor Dexter examined Dick rather critically, tapping his fingers on his desk. "Numbers and letters, you say?"

"Yes. It sounded like a cipher or some kind of code."

Dexter shook his head. "I can't understand it...What did Sende say?"

"Nothing. I'm not sure whether he had just left the shack or not."

Dexter made an abrupt movement. "I'll look into it tomorrow. There's nothing we can do tonight. Sende may know something about the matter, and if so, I'll find out." He tapped his fingers ruminatively. "I think that you'd better keep your discovery to yourself, at least till your father returns. Then the responsibility is his." He rose to his feet. "There's nothing we can do tonight, and you might as well get your sleep."

Dick reluctantly returned to his room, although as Professor Dexter had said, there was nothing that could be done that night. He undressed slowly and went to bed. As an afterthought he arose, locked the door, and returned to bed. He fell into a troubled doze, to be awakened by a slight sound. He jerked open his eyes, stared at the door knob. Was it his imagination, or did the knob slowly twist back to normal position? He sat up, stared at the door, but there was no recurrence of the sound or the motion. Long minutes later, stiff and sore from his fight with Hutchings, tense from his vigil, he sank back onto his bed.

How long he lay awake he was not sure; he had no awareness of falling asleep, but when next he awoke and looked at his watch, it was eight o'clock and time for breakfast; he had overslept.

He washed his face, dressed and hurried down to the mess hall. Hutchings, sitting hunched in a corner, darted him an evil glance through his discolored eye. Dick ignored him, took a seat.

Croft and Matucevitch, staff astronomers, sat across from him. Dick, absorbed in his own thoughts, was not conscious of their muttered conversation until Croft nudged him. "You came over from Venus on the *African Star*, didn't you, Dick?"

"Yes, what about it?"

Croft looked at him queerly. "'What about it,' he asks. Where have you been all morning?"

"I slept late. What happened to the *African Star*?"

Matucevitch said shortly, "She's had it."

Dick sat rigid. "The Basilisk?"

Croft nodded. "We intercepted the SOS. Just a few words, according to Sende. Something like, 'Attacked by pirate ship. Help…' And that was all."

# CHAPTER IX

## Blood on the Moon

DICK RETURNED TO HIS ROOM, lay on the bed with his hands behind his head. He thought of the familiar faces aboard the *African Star*: Captain Henshaw, Henry the erudite bosun, the pretty stewardess. All of them dead, horribly killed by the explosion of their own bodies. Hateful, detestable, vile, the Basilisk! Grief and rage almost choked Dick. He clenched his fingers; if only he held a gun and the Basilisk sat across the room from him! The Basilisk! Dick said the words to himself over and over, almost savoring his own hate. But there was more than hate — there was fear. The Basilisk suddenly seemed more real, more powerful and terrible than ever before; a figure looming like a great cloud over the observatory.

He must be a madman, thought Dick, if he were a man. He considered the personality of the Basilisk: there was cunning — reckless, daring, cruelty so intense as to suggest inhumanity. And Dick thought, was inhumanity entirely impossible? Certainly among the millions and billions of stars there were other intelligent races; why should not such creatures live even closer to home? He considered Crazy Sam's lunar natives. Was it possible that Crazy Sam was right and the entire phalanx of Earth scientists at fault? Stranger things had happened. The voice that had spoken the stealthy message over the radio had been unmistakably human; undoubtedly human beings were associated with the Basilisk, whether or not he himself were a man.

Dick rose to his feet, went to his radio, switched it on. Silence.

Nothing whatever on the air. He took up the paper on which he had copied the letters and numbers on the previous night's broadcast. Certainly it was a cipher of some sort, and in the hands of an expert cryptologist might well be deciphered.

He considered the characters from the standpoint of such an expert. He knew that the most common letter in the English language was *e*; therefore, if the cipher were a simple substitution type, he might well expect to find one particular character occurring with considerably greater frequency than the others.

He seated himself at the table, listed each character with the number of times it occurred in the message, and so arrived at the following table.

| | | | | |
|---|---|---|---|---|
| A – 7 | I – 8 | Q – 3 | 0 – 22 | 8 – 24 |
| B – 5 | J – 6 | R – 8 | 1 – 26 | 9 – 27 |
| C – 4 | K – 5 | S – 4 | 2 – 29 | |
| D – 7 | L – 6 | T – 6 | 3 – 25 | |
| E – 7 | M – 7 | U – 5 | 4 – 20 | |
| F – 9 | N – 6 | V – 7 | 5 – 21 | |
| G – 5 | O – 8 | W – 6 | 6 – 26 | |
| H – 6 | P – 4 | X – 8 | 7 – 25 | |

As he inspected the table, he became more confused than ever. On the average, the numbers occurred three or four times as often as the letters. Y and Z did not occur at all. It was hard to believe the cipher to be one of simple substitution. Unless, of course, a letter in the clear message were represented by more than one character in the cipher.

Dick chewed on his pencil. Somehow this did not seem to be the case; the digits were too consistently numerous. He made a second table.

| | | |
|---|---|---|
| 2 occurs 29 times | F | occurs 9 times |
| 9 " 27 " | I, O, R, X | " 8 " |
| 1, 6 " 26 " | A, D, E, M, V | " 7 " |
| 3, 7 " 25 " | H, J, L, N, T, W | " 6 " |
| 8 " 24 " | B, G, K, U | " 5 " |
| 0 " 22 " | C, P, S | " 4 " |
| 5 " 21 " | Q | " 3 " |
| 4 " 20 " | | |

Hardly a typical pattern of letter frequency, he thought. The solution to the cipher undoubtedly lay in another method. He considered the original message again, and almost at once felt a little ridiculous. The pattern of the cipher was quite definite: three letters followed by five numbers. In all there were 147 letters and 245 numbers; so that even by a random selection of letters and numbers there was bound to be an average of 24 occurrences per digit and 6 occurrences per letter.

It seemed clear then that each grouping of three letters and five numbers represented a separate entity, of which there would be — Dick counted — forty-nine.

Forty-nine words or forty-nine letters? It was possible that each grouping pointed to or indicated a word in some standard work, such as the *New One-World Dictionary*. Something tickled the back of Dick's mind. He studied the first group: RGA66953. Where had he seen such an assortment of letters and numbers? It had been quite recently. He had a sudden impression of dark shadows, subdued light, a rich, resonant voice. Dick sprang to his feet. Isel Bayer and his star index!

In new excitement he scrutinized his list of numbers. If he were correct, each of the forty-nine groups represented a star. Slowly he sat back down, feeling a little inadequate and wishing that his father were at the observatory. He looked at his watch and the calendar. Still almost four days until his father's return.

Dick made a neat copy of the message and put it in his pocket. He stood in the middle of the room a moment or two thinking; should he ask Professor Dexter's help or not?

He shrugged; there was no reason why it should be necessary. Isel Bayer had seemed to take his interest in the star index for granted; he would presumably see nothing odd in Dick's asking to examine the volumes at first hand.

Dick went downstairs to the library, but to his surprise Bayer refused point-blank to allow the star index out of his own hands. As he knotted his thin white fingers into his mop of fluffy white hair, he said peevishly: "There's too much work gone into this index to give it out to every Tom, Dick and Harry who ask for it. If you can put forward a sound and scientific reason for requiring it, then I have nothing to say;

but thumbing it over out of idle curiosity, no. There are better books for that kind of use."

"But I have a good reason!" protested Dick.

Isel Bayer turned the disks of the dark glasses full at him. "And what might this reason be?"

Dick stuttered and stammered, but could find no plausible pretext for wishing to look at the books.

"If you have any questions pertaining to the stars," said Bayer in a biting tone, "you need but ask. I assure you I have a wide knowledge of the subject."

Dick rose to his feet. "If I get Professor Dexter's O.K. —"

Bayer nodded. "Then I have no choice. While your father is away, Professor Dexter is in charge." His tone suggested that, so far as he was concerned, Professor Dexter might well remain in charge.

Dick crossed the hall to Dexter's office and knocked. Dexter's dry voice said, "Come in." He turned in his chair as Dick came through the door. "Well, Dick?"

"Professor Dexter, I would like to consult the star index, but Professor Bayer refuses to allow it unless I get your permission."

Dexter considered him thoughtfully. "I can't see what harm you'd do to the star index."

"No, I don't intend to do any harm."

"Can't you put your problem to Professor Bayer? He'd be flattered and be glad to help."

"No," said Dick desperately. "I don't want to. It's rather a private affair. As a matter of fact, I'm trying to decode that message I heard last night."

"Oh!" Professor Dexter tapped his teeth. "I see, and you want to keep the nature of your investigation private?"

"Yes, that's it exactly."

"Well, quite right." He reached for the telephone. "I can't see any reason why you shouldn't have access to the star index." He nodded to Dick. "Go back to the library; I'll arrange the matter with Professor Bayer."

"You won't say anything of what I'm doing?" asked Dick.

"No, not a word."

When Dick returned to the library he found Sende standing in front of the desk, his head cocked down toward Professor Bayer like a poised ax.

Bayer said into the telephone, "Quite all right, Professor; certainly, quite all right." He turned to Dick, and there was a complete change in his manner.

"Well, well, Dick, Professor Dexter thinks it a good idea for you to study the star index, and I'm sure I can't see any reason why you shouldn't. Which volume do you want?"

"All of them, please."

"You can't take them from the library, you understand."

"I'll work at that far table."

Professor Bayer unlocked a cabinet and stood aside while Dick carried the index, three volumes at a time, to the far table.

"Anything else, Dick?"

"Well — I'd like a set of star charts."

"They're included in the index."

"Thank you." Conscious of the pressure of Sende's yellow eyes, Dick went to the table, spread out his notes and started to work.

Sende exchanged a few muttered sentences with Bayer and left the library.

The plan of the index was clear enough; after a moment Dick located the star corresponding to the first grouping of letters and numbers on his list. Unlike the immense majority of the stars indexed, this star bore a subsidiary title: Rho Ophiuchi. Dick thumbed the index to the second star, which proved to be Iota Sagittarii. Third star was nothing less than Alpha Lyrae, or Vega.

Certain now that he was on the track of significant information, he bent to his task with complete absorption. Grouping after grouping became a star, and each bore a parenthetical name from the older nomenclature. Forty-nine sets of characters became forty-nine stars.

Dick closed the last volume of the index with a deep sigh of satisfaction. A reflection on Isel Bayer's dark glasses caught his attention. He looked up, stared across the room a trifle defiantly. Bayer's head turned slightly, but Dick had the feeling that the eyes behind the shelter of the glasses were watching his every move. He returned uneasily to his work, keeping one eye on Bayer.

Then he opened the index to the master star chart and located the various stars, hoping to find some sort of pattern, but the results were inconclusive.

He sat back in his chair. Forty-nine stars. Somehow they were tied into the fate of the *African Star*.

The solution came to him in a blinding flash; how could he have been so dense not to have seen it immediately? The Greek letters formed the message: Rho Ophiuchi meant *R*; Iota Sagittarii was *I*; Alpha Lyrae was *A*; Kappa Ursae was *K*.

Dick hurriedly transcribed the entire message, hesitating only at Theta Orionis and Theta Gemini, both of which he transcribed *th*, and Phi Argo Navis, which he wrote *F*.

The complete message read:

RIKANSTARDEPONETHIRTYMONAKTOGFOUR
OURSIXTEENTHGKORSA

At first the deciphered message appeared as confusing as the original. But certain words were clear: 'star', 'one', 'thirty', 'four', 'our', 'sixteenth'.

He separated the known words, and the message became:

RIKAN STAR DEP ONE THIRTY MONAK TOG FOUR
OUR SIXTEENTH GKORSA.

Dick recalled that he had broken in upon the message; that he had missed part of it. Seen in this light RIKAN was clearly the last of "African," there being no Greek equivalent for the letter *C*.

Apparently, as he had suspected, the message concerned the *African Star*; evidently it dealt with the ship's course. In this case DEP might easily stand for 'departs'; and the MON after THIRTY was probably 'Monday'.

'*African Star* departs one-thirty Monday' now read the first half of the message. But what was AK TOG FOUR OUR SIXTEENTH GKORSA?

Dick puzzled half an hour without any enlightenment.

Isel Bayer rose to his feet, shot a glance at Dick, stalked from the room.

Dick laid down the paper, leaned back in his chair, stared up at the ceiling. Knowing the time of a spaceship's departure, what further information would be necessary before it could be located accurately in the vast empty reaches of space? Obviously, the direction it was headed and the speed with which it moved.

A spaceship's speed, however, changed every instant; acceleration was the significant factor. The word 'acceleration' was the key. Dick scanned the message, seized upon the letters AK — the abbreviation for 'acceleration'. His eyes leaped ahead to the letter G — 'gravity', and TO was 'two'. 'Acceleration two gravities, four—' OUR — must be 'hours', since the Greek H was not represented by a distinct symbol. Then 'sixteenth gravity'.

Now the departure and the acceleration were definite. KORSA could only refer to the course. 'Course A'? A might point either to some pre-determined code or it even — Dick looked back to his list — it might even mean 'in the direction of Alpha Scorpionis', or Antares. But it made little difference; the essence of his discovery was that someone either at the observatory or nearby was broadcasting information re-garding spaceships leaving Earth, to persons unknown, presumably the Basilisk.

Dick carefully folded his papers, placed them in his pocket. Profes-sor Bayer had not yet returned to the library, so Dick carried the books back to the case and carefully replaced them.

He started up to his room, then hesitated. At this moment he did not care to be alone. He looked toward Professor Dexter's room, started forward, hesitated, and decided to keep his knowledge to himself until his father returned. There was no one he could trust; everyone at the observatory was open to suspicion, Dexter included.

He went down to the lounge, where he found Crazy Sam striding impatiently back and forth, muttering to himself. "Promised me two new jets, Doc Murdock did," he said in an aggrieved voice to Dick. "Told me plain as day I could have 'em to fix my little ore cart. And now Old Fiddlesticks — can't think of his name — tells me nothing doing. What do you think of that, boy?" And he gave Dick a piercing look. Apparently he had forgotten his quarrel with Dick.

"I suppose as soon as my father comes home you'll get your jets."

Crazy Sam clapped Dick's shoulder with his horny old hand. "That's it, my boy — now why don't I think of those things myself? All I do is wait. Old Fiddlesticks — whatever his name is — can be blowed! And now, what do you say to going out on a little prospecting trip, hey?"

Dick thought immediately of the ledge where he had found the purple crystal. "I'd like to go very much."

"Well, get your suit on then, and we'll be off. Out across Lake Baxter into the Badlands."

"Two shakes," said Dick. "I've got to let Professor Dexter know where I'm going."

He ran upstairs to Professor Dexter's office, knocked, and then entered at the crisp summons.

As usual, Dexter was seated at his desk and barely looked up when Dick crossed the room. "Yes, Dick?"

"Crazy Sam wants me to go prospecting with him. I thought I'd better tell you, in view of what you said yesterday."

Dexter nodded. "You're safe with Crazy Sam; be sure to check your oxygen."

"Yes sir." Dick raced back downstairs. Crazy Sam was in the ward room, already pulling on his space-suit.

Ten minutes later the rickety rocket-raft lurched off into the airless lunar sky. The crater with the observatory diminished behind; the tortured black sea of lava spread out to the horizons. Ahead towered Baxter Point; they passed by, slanted down over an expanse which Crazy Sam grandly described as "Mare Baxteria — all of it, east to west."

Glancing over his shoulder, Dick thought he saw a shadow flitting down over Baxter Point, now behind them. He strained his eyes, but if a flying object were there, it could no longer be seen among the angled ridges and the midnight shadows.

Far to the left Dick spied a shape he thought he recognized. "Is that Baxter Mesa over there?" he asked.

"Right you are, Baxter Mesa it is."

"Let's go back to that ledge; I'd like to get a few more tourmalines."

"No sooner said than done." Sam swung the raft around. Baxter Mesa grew larger and larger. Below them opened the Baxter Bottomless Pit, ahead was the ledge with the tourmalines.

Crazy Sam landed the raft, jumped off. "Here we are, fine as velvet, the best tourmalines on the moon twenty feet away from you." He seemed in excellent spirits. Then, as if he had recalled the incident of the parchment chart, he ostentatiously raised the toolbox lid. "Nothing there, my lad; no spying this time." He chuckled. "Now, now." He waved his hand as Dick started to protest. "I'm willing to admit it was an accident, but Crazy Sam don't let accidents happen twice. Now get busy, find yourself a bucket of tourmaline, and then we'll be off and I'll show you some real jewels."

Dick laughed. "Do you want to see some real jewels? Come with me — I'll show *you* some." He started down the ledge to the spot where he had found the flaming purple crystal, and Sam hopped behind, obviously puzzled. "What's all this now?"

"Just watch," said Dick.

Where the black sill slanted through the porphyry, he raised his pick, began to dig.

"Just what you going after, son?" asked Sam in a curious voice.

Dick, turning his head to answer, happened by merest chance to glance upward. His voice rattled in his throat; he screamed, "Look out!" and flung himself to the side.

A black shape grew larger, larger, smashed into the ledge exactly where he had been standing — a tremendous black boulder. The ledge shattered, a flake of rock sprang out into space, the boulder bounded after it.

A horrible cry sounded in Dick's ears, rattling the speaker. He saw Sam floundering in the emptiness, fighting, kicking the boulder which had thrust him out. Slowly at first, then faster and faster, Sam dropped. He disappeared into the blackness of Baxter's Bottomless Pit, but his terrified yelling sounded in Dick's ears as he fell. Then there was utter silence...

# CHAPTER X

## *The Thing with the Golden Eyes*

DICK STOOD PRESSING BACK against the porphyry of the cliff so hard that he felt the stone through the fabric of his space-suit. His eyes bulged from their sockets, his fingers made sweaty creases in the woolen inner gloves, his mouth was locked open and his tongue was dry. Blood returned slowly to his brain, his knees loosened, his mouth closed and his chest heaved in a series of racking gasps. And through the first paralysis of sensation came a flood of fear — personal terror. The hurtling boulder might have been an accident, but Dick was under no illusions. It was timed too perfectly, aimed too exactly. And now two questions — or rather a single great fear with two separate aspects — came to his mind: had the boulder been intended for Sam or for himself? And if Sam had been an accidental victim, would the assassin drop down to the ledge to make sure of Dick?

He drew himself carefully along the ledge, pressing close as a shadow to the stone, and so reached the shelter of an overhanging jut. From the darkness he peered up toward the lip of the cliff, and it was all he could do to control his hopelessness and terror. An adversary he could see — a man, an animal — would have been a relief. But an unseen creature that hurled boulders down the cliff, who or what could it be? A lunar native, the Basilisk himself?

Dick recalled the shape he had glimpsed flitting down through the shadows of Baxter Range, and part of his composure returned. It was clear that someone was bent on killing him; probably because he had heard and deciphered the secret radio message.

Dick gritted his teeth. He should have used more caution. It would have been wiser to wait until Isel Bayer was asleep, then by hook or by crook gain entrance to the library. But there was no use crying over spilled milk; the damage was done.

Anxiously he looked up along the face of the cliff. No motion, nothing strange or alarming. And yet something up there had rolled a great boulder over the edge which had missed him by a yard. Dick's flesh crawled at the recollection.

He waited another five minutes then, keeping well back in the shadows, inched along the ledge to a ragged gash in the cliff, which offered an easy series of steps to the top of the mesa. Inside this ravine he was more or less hidden from anyone above; he cast caution aside, sprang up the rocks in great thirty-foot leaps. He reached the top of the notch and peered across the flat surface. It was bare as a clean plate.

He scanned the sky. Far toward the horizon he thought he caught the blue glimmer of jets; he strained his eyes, but among the flaming multitude of stars, certainty was impossible.

He ran across the mesa, looked down at the ledge. Crazy Sam's old raft lay forlorn and lonesome directly below. Dick turned back to the top of the plateau. Where had the boulder come from? A hundred yards away was a broken clutter of rock. Looking closely, Dick spied scratches in the naked face of the mesa. Beyond question the boulder had been rolled or dragged from its bed, aimed, dropped.

Black wilderness stretched in all directions; lunar crags stabbed toward the face of Earth. And down in the Bottomless Pit lay the body of Crazy Sam Baxter. Dick shivered, then clenched his teeth. A nerve-wracking but unavoidable task lay ahead of him.

He returned to the ledge, gingerly approached Sam's old raft, as if it were indeed the skittish Bronco Bert. He settled himself on the forward bench, jiggled the joy stick. The four jets swiveled obediently. He held the joy stick perfectly vertical, turned the master valve. Oxygen and hydrogen pouring into the jets roared into flame. The raft quivered, bounced. He eased open the valve; the raft floated up. He pushed the joy stick a fraction of an inch to the side; the raft drifted out over the

Bottomless Pit. He straightened the joy stick, closed the master valve a hair; the raft settled.

Rock walls rose level with his eyes, reared over his head. The jets cast an eery light on the glassy cliff face, on which no human eye had ever gazed before.

Dick sat rigid, tense, as if his bones were steel and his muscles whale-bone. Between his legs he could look down into the dark void; to either side the crevasse walls loomed, closing slowly in, slowly pinching at the raft.

Claustrophobia, fear of being pent and constricted, flickered up through his brain; suppose the walls should suddenly come together? He would be pressed flat, like a gnat in a book. He grimaced, pushed the morbid imaginings back from his mind.

Down, down, down, and a hypnotic pressure began to build up in his brain. Flaring jets, glistening gray rock, walls sliding noiselessly up past him, attention riveted into the darkness under him. Down, down, down — into the Bottomless Pit.

How long, how far, how deep? He never knew; the descent was like a dream. But at some unknown time stone glimmered directly below, and Dick sank down like waterlogged flotsam to the floor of a dark ocean. And there — a sprawled shape in the ghostly light — was the shattered and air-blown body of Crazy Sam Baxter.

Dick cushioned the shock of landing with an extra bit of power, then closed the valve entirely. Darkness clapped on his shoulders like a load of black wool. Utter silence, utter darkness, utter loneliness.

Thrilling in every nerve, walking with a peculiar feeling of being at once completely alive and yet only half awake, Dick groped for Sam's body. He felt it, yielding and loose. On Earth Sam would have weighed no more than a hundred and forty pounds; on the moon Dick was able to lift him with one hand.

Thankful now for the dark, he carried the body back, set it on the back bench. Then seating himself once more in the pilot's seat, he opened the master valve and began the long ascent.

The crack of sky at the top of the chasm became a trickle of stars across the blackness, gradually widening to a rivulet, a path, a band, and finally, as the raft roared out into clear space, the glorious spangled vault.

Dick pushed the joy stick ahead, tilting the jets backward, and now the raft went through the same series of swoops, dips and bounding ascents that had plagued Sam. But Dick soon fastened upon a technique which Sam, for all his experience, had apparently never learned. He opened the master valve to almost full power, then as the raft shot upward, hauled slowly back on the joy stick until the raft sped in level flight across the terrain.

Back over the now familiar landmarks: Mare Baxteria, Baxter Point, Lake Baxter. And there, glowing in the Earthlight like an alabaster carving, was the observatory, with the big telescope perched on the crater like a toy.

Dick heaved a great sigh. Another five minutes and his responsibility was at its end; Sam's battered old body would be given a decent burial, and presumably another caretaker appointed to the Security Station... Something clicked in Dick's mind. The chart! Where was the chart, the tangle of red and blue lines of which Sam had been so sensitive? Not in the toolbox certainly...

Dick chewed his lip. If he landed inside the observatory square and if the chart were on Sam's person, there was no telling who would take custody of the mysterious bit of parchment. There was only one course open — a grisly bit of business, but necessary if the chart had significance other than that offered by the warp in Sam's mind.

Instead of landing inside the observatory square, Dick lowered the raft to a flat table of lava on the other side of the crater wall. There, unobserved, he started to search Sam's space-suit.

Sam, surprisingly enough, wore no outside pouch, and Dick thought this very strange; he had a clear mental picture of the little bag swinging at Sam's side when he jumped aboard the rocket-raft. But the pouch was nowhere in evidence, and Dick convinced himself that he had been mistaken.

The chart was not concealed on Sam's space-suit. Dick trembled in distaste at what he must do. There was no help for it; so he steeled himself to the task. He unzipped Sam's space-suit far enough to search the pockets of Sam's clothes. He found nothing. The chart was not on Sam's body.

Dick turned back to the raft. He ransacked the tool box. Nothing.

He looked under the bench, under the jet struts. Nothing. The chart was not on Sam or on the raft.

Where was it then? He could picture only one other possibility: Sam's isolated little dwelling near the Security Station.

Dick once more took the raft into the air, slid over the crater wall and settled into the observatory square.

Trusting no one, Dick reported Sam's death as an accident. Sam, he said, had incautiously pried loose the boulder which had flung him back into the chasm. Professor Dexter, not completely satisfied, questioned Dick keenly, and under the thrust of the brilliant black eyes Dick had stammered and stumbled. He was not naturally a good liar, and Professor Dexter's evident suspicion made deception even more difficult.

At the end of the inquisition Professor Dexter became a trifle sarcastic, and stared at Dick with his fine black eyebrows in a dissatisfied line. "Your father will be home in a few days; I'll make a report to him and I'm sure he'll want to make a thorough investigation."

Dick nodded, blushing.

"That's all then," Dexter said rather sharply.

Dick left the office and went up to his room. Professor Dexter's suspicion weighed on him a great deal less than the knowledge that somewhere among the personnel of the observatory was a heartless murderer, an ally of the pirates and a traitor to civilized humanity. The idea had developed in Dick's mind to near-certainty. In theory it was possible that the stealthy radio message had been broadcast elsewhere, that a pirate spy had followed Crazy Sam's boat to the Baxter Mesa and there, from sheer malevolence, dropped a boulder — but it was highly unlikely.

Where was the chart? Sam may have been cantankerous, outspoken and queer, but a streak of common sense seemed to lie underneath. If he had snatched the chart out from under Dick's eyes, Dick felt sure that the chart had significance.

But nothing was certain. The chart might mean nothing, or it might be highly important; at any rate, its absence gnawed at Dick's nerves. He paced up and down his room, stopping at the window every two or three trips. Off to the side lay Sam's old raft, forlorn and neglected. And every time Dick came to the window he looked longer at the raft.

Conflicting impulses worked at Dick's brain. His nerves were jangling, and he was frightened. Close by was his enemy, a person who would kill him with satisfaction. Any footstep outside his door might well be this enemy... Almost with the thought, he fancied he heard a footstep; he paused in his pacing and listened. The sound was not repeated. Quietly he crossed the room and locked the door.

Dick looked at the bed; he was tired, but he knew he could not sleep. He wanted to act, strike out, fight back. It was humiliating to be forced to stand and numbly take punishment; he walked back and forth with quicker strides. Sam's raft beckoned him; the sky was bright with blazing stars, clearer than any sky of Earth. Once on the raft, and on his guard, he could detect anyone who might try to follow him a second time. Of course Professor Dexter had definitely instructed him to go nowhere alone; but if he were caught, he could suffer no more than a sharp lecture, and if worse came to worst he could explain his actions. He knew his father would understand and possibly even approve; Professor Dexter was more steely and intense, a great deal less flexible.

Dick shrugged; he would cross the bridge of Professor Dexter's disapproval when he came to it.

He paused before the locked door; suppose someone were standing on the other side waiting? He picked up the heaviest object in sight — a tall bottle of after-shave lotion, quietly unlocked the door, and with a beating heart flung it open.

The corridor was empty.

Dick returned the lotion to its place on the shelf and ran downstairs. He slid unobserved into his space-suit, replaced his oxygen tank, and the process gave him pause for thought. The raft would likewise need refueling. Well, he'd take it across the square and fill the tanks himself; Lobscombe, the electrolysis engineer — Lobscouse, as Crazy Sam had called him — was round-headed and stubborn; persuasion and argument would get nowhere with Lobscombe.

Dick moved swiftly, efficiently. He hopped aboard the raft, opened the master valve. In the throat of the jets, little catalyzer plates automatically ignited the oxygen and hydrogen. The raft rose, and under his now knowledgeable hand, looped easily across the square, settled beside the fuel outlets.

Dick jumped off hastily. His only hope was to get well underway before Lobscombe appeared. But he was in luck, and he filled the tanks without interruption. A moment later he was riding up and away from the observatory, across the cruel black wilderness of the lava sea.

He kept careful watch behind him, but there was no pursuit. To make doubly sure he dropped suddenly into a lonely little crater and waited fifteen minutes. Nothing in sight but dim-lit rock, black shadow, and the infinite spread of the universe above.

Confident now that he had evaded his enemy, Dick flew toward the old Security Station. Miles slipped under him, together with a thousand craters, black crevasses, monstrous mountains. Then in the distance appeared the pallid ruins. At another time Dick would have enjoyed exploring the battered old hangars and warehouses; this time he had a definite end in view — searching Crazy Sam's dwelling. He saw it, an igloo-shaped dome a half-mile distant from the ruins.

He dropped the raft, jumped off and ran to the door. The quicker he finished his job the better.

He had no difficulty in gaining entrance, and two minutes after landing he stood among Crazy Sam's meager belongings. Several items gave him considerable surprise: an easel, a much-used palette, brushes and tubes of oil paints. On the walls hung a dozen moonscapes depicting the moon as Sam had seen it: a place of brooding solitude and immeasurable antiquity.

Dick hurriedly started to work. First he opened Sam's old sea chest of carved teak. It contained nothing but canister after canister of rank black tobacco, and in the corner half a dozen bottles of liquor.

Dick went to the wardrobe, and here his search was short; Sam's only outfit seemed to be the one on his back. Next he rummaged through the desk, which was cluttered with crystals of all shapes and colors, a fortune twenty times over. But Dick had no interest in dead stones; he brushed them impatiently aside in his search.

He tore open the bed, pounded the pillow. Nothing. He looked into Sam's stove, searched the cans and sacks of food, peered down the sink and bathroom drains. Nothing. He looked behind the pictures on the wall. Nothing.

He glanced into the trash basket, where he found a crumpled ball of paper. He picked it out, smoothed it. It bore a picture scratched in colored pencil. The superscription read, 'Drawn from life, by Sam Baxter.' The picture showed a spindly manlike creature. A black cloak hung from thin shoulders past thin knees. The head was covered by a broad-rimmed black hat. The eyes were large as grapefruit, golden-yellow with hypnotic black centers. The face was inhuman, expressionless, full of the strange elemental power which sometimes radiates from enlarged photographs of insect heads. The picture, crude as it was, was compelling; Dick could hardly move his eyes. A hurried scrawl slanted across the bottom — "'Basilisk' is as good a name as any."

# CHAPTER XI

## The Basilisk Stirs

DICK TORE HIS GAZE from the crude picture, and the effort was like pulling his feet out of sucking mud. With quivering fingers he folded it, tucked it into his pouch. He made a last hasty survey of the dome, but now it was full of the golden-eyed presence, and Dick pushed out through the air lock as if he were escaping suffocation.

He jumped aboard the raft, opened the master valve wide, hauled hard back on the joy stick, and the raft skidded up into the air like a dart from a catapult.

Without incident he returned to the observatory and parked the raft in an inconspicuous corner of the square. To his relief, no one appeared to have noticed his absence; even Hutchings did no more than give him a surly look as he passed through the lounge.

Dick slid the folded picture of the Basilisk into a pigeonhole in his father's desk and then washed his hands, as if he had been handling something foul.

He looked at his watch — half an hour till suppertime. He changed from his casual clothes — loose blue trousers and pullover — to gray slacks and a dark jacket, and sauntered downstairs, through the lounge and along the passage to the mess hall.

He was a few minutes early; taking a seat by the wall, he watched the observatory personnel file in. By this time faces and names were connecting together. He recognized Croft, Matucevitch and Bauer, astronomers, Peterson the gardener, Rapotsky the ice miner, Carter and Meriot, laboratory technicians, currently doing research with silicone compounds at absolute-zero temperatures.

One by one the seats filled up. Dick saw the steward carry out a tray destined either for Professor Dexter or Isel Bayer, neither of whom had put in an appearance. Looking around the mess hall, Dick saw that Sende also was absent. He toyed with the idea of running back to his room and turning on his radio, and just as he was wavering in his seat, Sende came into the room.

He stood in the doorway, looking from face to face; Dick covertly studied the hard profile. He thought, a person could hold a sickle up and the curve would fit smoothly around Sende's face.

The bony head turned; Sende came forward, striding purposefully across the room. He sank into the chair opposite Dick, tossed a folded sheet of yellow paper across. "For you. Just came by trans-space radio."

Dick opened the paper with nervous fingers; it could only be from his father, and could only be bad news.

Bad news it was indeed.

"Dear Dick: Received notification via trans-space that Mother is desperately ill at Lake Oriens: Tchobelov's Virus. She is not expected to live. I am catching the *Australian Star* for Venus. Please pack a few Venus clothes for me, bring my personal briefcase, join me tomorrow aboard the ship. If we're lucky, we'll arrive in time. Father."

Dick sat for a moment, stunned. Blinking back the tears he read the message again, looked up at Sende, who sat watching him with impersonal interest.

Dick struggled to master his voice. "What time does the dispatch boat go up to meet the *Australian Star*?"

"Early," said Sende. "Seven o'clock sharp."

Soup was set in front of him. Dick ate automatically, without hunger. Life was suddenly gray and dull; even the Basilisk seemed unimportant. He bent his head to hide his brimming eyes; the food choked in his throat. He rose to his feet, went swiftly to his room, where he flung himself on his bed.

Tchobelov's Virus — commonly known as Black Crawler Disease, from the ribbons of infection forming in the body — was almost always fatal, and no cure was known. His father had never used the colloquial expression, preferring the rather formal term 'Tchobelov's Virus'; by this token Dick was certain the message was genuine.

The idea, which apparently had been wandering unspoken in his subconscious, aroused a second train of thought. Granted that his father's message was genuine, was it altogether certain that the message from Venus was the same?

Dick sat up on his bed. Suddenly the whole idea seemed odd. In the first place, immediately after Dick's departure his mother had left for their summer home on the slopes of Mount Colossus in the far north. Dick was sure of this; the plans had been made for a month. Furthermore, no Venusian resident in his right mind would visit Lake Oriens in the steaming Venusian summer. And thirdly, Dick's mother had lived sixteen years on Venus; by all the past experience of the Earth settlers she should have acquired an immunity to Tchobelov's Virus; it attacked only newcomers from Earth, and this peculiarity made it very rare.

He jumped to his feet, started to run down to the radio shack. But no message would reach his father now. Dick halted, slowly returned to the bed, sat down...What could be the motive of such a cruel message? A ruse to get his father away from the observatory? Or was there a grimmer purpose to the plot? Suppose the *Australian Star* were slated for attack? The message then might well be an instrument luring his father, and Dick along with him, to their deaths.

What could be the purpose behind these careful stratagems? How would the Basilisk profit by the death of Dr. Murdock? Dick knew his father to be that rare specimen, a brilliant scientist and an efficient organizer, but certainly he was not indispensable, and Professor Dexter could no doubt fill his shoes satisfactorily. Perhaps Professor Dexter would go next, and then who would head the observatory? Isel Bayer? Dick's father had mentioned such a possibility.

Dick went thoughtfully from his room down the stairs to Professor Dexter's office. He knocked, but there was no response. Dick continued down to the lounge, where he paced restlessly back and forth for twenty minutes.

Through the window he saw five men coming from the direction of the telescope; as they drew near he saw them to be Professor Dexter,

Isel Bayer, Bauer, Matucevitch and Sende. Five minutes later they entered the lounge. Sende stalked silently off down the passageway to the radio shack, Isel Bayer climbed the stairs toward the library, Dexter stood giving terse instructions to Bauer and Matucevitch.

Dick waited until the two astronomers had moved away, then approached Professor Dexter. "May I speak to you a moment?"

Dexter turned his head. "What's the trouble?"

"It's this." Dick handed him the trans-space message.

Professor Dexter read the message. "That's too bad," he said shortly. He shot Dick one of his sharp side glances. "I imagine you'll be going up on the dispatch boat."

"Yes." Dick started to speak, hesitated, then the words came in a flood. "There's something unbelievable about the whole situation. I don't think my mother is sick; it's just that someone wants to get my father on the *Australian Star*."

Dexter was silent for a moment. Then he said slowly, "Your father would hardly let a false message deceive him."

"I don't know," said Dick miserably. "I think he'd be so worried that he wouldn't think much about anything."

"Well," said Dexter, "there's nothing you can do at the moment. I can't think of anything to suggest unless it's that you get a good night's sleep."

Dick nodded rather forlornly, turned away. He went up to his room, stared out the window at Earth, tracing the blue-gray-green continents so familiar from books and maps, but on which he had never set foot: Asia, Africa, the complex little peninsula of Europe. His father would even now be aboard the *Australian Star*, speeding across the gulf. And somewhere the Basilisk's grim ships drifted, waiting for a signal…

Dick went to his radio, flicked the switch. Nothing sounded but the hum of the tubes. He turned out the lights, lay on his bed and presently fell into a troubled doze.

A voice awakened him: a voice crisp, resonant, and at the same time muffled. Dick raised up on the bed, blinking. Who could be talking in the middle of the night? He sprang to his feet. The radio! He raced to the desk, began copying letters and numbers.

The voice snapped off. Dick jumped up, started for the door, but remembering his previous lack of success, came to a frustrated halt. He clenched his fists in vexation; if only, instead of stopping to copy the message, he had run down to the radio shack, he might have caught the spy in the act!

He looked down at the list of symbols, wondering what might be their meaning. At least he now knew the secret of the cipher; it would require only half an hour to work out the clear message.

He started for the door, hesitated. Instinct told him to move stealthily, with the most painstaking caution; someone at the observatory would resent interference. Dick listened at the door. Silence. He looked at his watch. After three o'clock; no one would be abroad at this hour. He unlocked the door, opened it a crack, peered down the corridor; it was deserted. He stepped out, stole quietly along the passage, down the steps, padded to the library.

The little strip of pebbled glass over the door was dark; Isel Bayer was either in his bed, at the telescope, or abroad on schemes of his own. Dick slipped inside and, since there was no help for it, turned on the lights.

Now he must move rapidly. He went to the cabinet which housed the star index. Locked. Dick wasted not an instant. He picked a book from the shelf, rapped the glass smartly. The glass broke, fell to the floor with a clatter that Dick felt must rouse the observatory. But no stopping now. He put his hand in the hole, caught hold of the door frame, pulled. The lock snapped, the door swung open.

Dick pulled the books down to the table. If Isel Bayer objected, he could make his complaints to Dr. Murdock, and Dick knew that his father would defend his actions.

He got busy. The message was a trifle longer than the first, and an hour went by before he had the clear message in front of him. Correcting the spelling, the message read: '*Australian Star* leaves moon for Venus, seven-thirty today. Course unknown. Must.'

'Must —' Must attack? Must kill? And 'course unknown'. The Basilisk would wait in the dark gulf close by the moon. He would center the *Australian Star* on his radar, trail it out into the Graveyard. Then the approach, the close-in for the kill; the rocket spitting across space, exploding into the bridge. The ship's air would gush out into the vacuum; air inside the passenger's bodies would bubble and swell, fifteen pounds for every square inch of skin. Men, women, children would pop open like deep-sea fish brought to the surface.

Dick returned to the last word. 'Must'. Ambiguous, significant. Must what? Actually Dick needed no answer. The sense behind the word was all too clear.

Dr. Murdock must be killed.

Rage burned and trembled inside Dick. His father represented everything that was good: kindness, tolerance, humor, unselfishness. And these creatures, men who had lost the right to call themselves men, wished to erase his father's life! If the chance ever came to him, Dick vowed that he would be as cruel and merciless as the pirates. He gritted his teeth in frustration, aching to strike back at the Basilisk.

He looked at his watch, and with a start of surprise, saw that it was almost five o'clock. Morning. In another two hours the dispatch boat left to meet the *Australian Star*. Sende would be piloting; if he were the spy, would he allow Dick to board the spaceship? Dick groaned for a weapon, a gun. But there was no such object at the observatory; what could anyone shoot in the airless desolation of rock and lava?

Dick considered further. If Sende were the spy, he would know that the *Australian Star* was destined to destruction and would care little whether Dick boarded the ship or not. If Dick had read his sardonic personality right, he would be a trifle amused; Dick might expect to find him especially courteous on the way out.

Dick jumped grimly to his feet, went to the door. The door was locked. He twisted the knob in annoyance. Locked. Some officious busybody had locked him in...Some officious busybody or—He stood back, considered the door with new eyes. It was strong metal, the lock was strong. In two hours the dispatch boat left to meet the *Australian Star*—and with it would go his last chance to save his father.

# Chapter XII

## Human Satellite

Dick's first thought was to kick the door open. But it swung inward, and he might as well have kicked at the wall. The blows, however, did produce noise, and Dick continued to kick in hope of attracting attention. After a few minutes he used a chair to beat on the panels, producing even more noise. He aroused no one. The second-floor corridor, when he paused to press his ear to the door, was as silent as a tomb. With a feeling close to panic he redoubled his efforts, stopping only when his breath failed.

Still no response. Dick sat down heavily. He was helpless, caught like an animal in a trap; if he did not get out, he would have failed his father. Failed. The word galvanized him; he couldn't fail. Failure meant death for his father. He rubbed his temples, forced himself to think calmly.

How could he communicate with someone outside? The answer was so obvious that he sat for a moment full of anger at his own stupidity. The intercommunication system.

He went to Bayer's desk, flicked the switch, pressed the button that would ring Professor Dexter's unit. There was no answer; the speaker emitted not so much as a hum. Dick pressed the mess-hall button; at this hour someone would be in the kitchen. No answer; the speaker was dead.

In growing anxiety Dick pushed button after button — no answer. He pounded the speaker, jiggled the switch. Useless. It was evident that the instrument had been disengaged from the circuit at the main switchboard.

Dick slowly returned to the center of the room. Wild ideas stampeded through his brain. He could break open a window; air would puff out of the library, pressure would blow the door open. Of course he would be dead long before.

He looked at his watch. Six o'clock. Sixty more minutes. He lunged at the door, kicking, pounding with his fists until he was exhausted. He rested a minute, then picking up the chair began to beat out a steady SOS in Morse code; surely someone must hear.

His arms ached. It seemed as if he had been standing here tapping at the door all his life. He stopped, listened. Silence outside. Six twenty-five. Grimly he set to work again. *Tap-tap-tap. Tap — tap — tap. Tap-tap-tap.* Over and over.

There was a sound outside, a step. Dick cried, "Open the door, let me out!"

After a moment of silence, a voice said cautiously, "Who is in there?"

Dick recognized the voice; it belonged to Mervin Hutchings. "It's me, Dick Murdock! Open up!"

Hutchings laughed. "How did you lock yourself in?"

"I didn't; someone locked me in. Hurry, let me out. I've got to catch the dispatch boat."

Hutchings' laugh came again. "Stay there and rot for all I care. I didn't lock you in."

"I've got to get up to the *Australian Star*!" cried Dick. "My father's aboard; the pirates are going to attack it!"

"Pooh," came Hutchings' voice. "Don't give me pirate talk; I don't get taken in by that storybook stuff."

"I tell you it's the truth; let me out!"

"Nope," said Hutchings smugly. "Your father told me to keep an eye on you, but you're an evasive little rat. Now I know where you are, and it's a good place for you. Right now I'm going down to breakfast. Why don't you take a nap until old cotton-head Bayer shows up?"

Dick cried out, "No, no — let me out!" But in vain. He heard Hutchings' footsteps receding down the corridor.

As close to hysteria as he had ever been, Dick picked up the chair once more, pounded, rapped, harder and harder, until the chair cracked and broke.

Panting, sweating, Dick looked at his watch. Ten minutes to seven... I've got to get out, he thought. He took another chair, began pounding once more. Harder and harder; as the minute hand crept toward twelve he thought of Hutchings, and rage boiled up inside him. He thought of his father aboard the doomed spaceship, and the strength seemed to flow from his muscles, leaving them lax as wet string.

One minute to seven. He raised his head wildly. Voices in the corridor? He picked up the chair, pounded on the now scarred and battered door.

He heard muttered ejaculations of surprise, then the sound of approaching footsteps. "Who's that in there?" came a measured crisp voice — Professor Dexter's.

"It's me, Dick. I'm locked in."

There was the jingle of keys, the rattle of metal in the lock. The door swung open. Professor Dexter and Isel Bayer stood in the doorway. Bayer, after one look at the broken cabinet, the smashed chairs, bayed, "You young hooligan, what's the meaning of this?"

Dexter looked at Dick with a peculiar quizzical expression. "I thought you were going up on the dispatch boat?"

"I was locked in," cried Dick, pushing past them. "I've been here four hours; has it gone yet?"

Dexter looked at his wrist watch. "I'm not sure; if you hurry you might be able to make it."

Dick ran along the corridor, vaulted pell-mell downstairs, crossed the lounge into the ward room. Through the window he glimpsed the boat, with Sende already in the cabin. He climbed into his space-suit, saying over and over to himself, "Make him wait, make him wait, make him wait." His fingers disobeyed his brain; he fumbled with the zippers, jammed the seal-rings. Taking no time to check his supply of oxygen, he ran into the double-lock, started the pump.

Seconds passed, dragging like minutes. Dick pressed against the door. The air was exhausted; the door opened. Jumping out upon the crater floor, Dick came to a dead halt. The boat had gone. The square was empty. High in the black sky shone the blue glimmer of the four jets.

Dick wanted to scream, to cry, to pound his fists on the ground. It would have gone ill with Hutchings had he appeared at this moment.

Dick forced himself to stand perfectly still, to think. Was there no way to communicate with the *Australian Star*? The radio shack would be locked, with Sende in the dispatch boat; it was doubtful if anyone else could operate the equipment. No, it was up to him; it was unthinkable that he should not be able to save his father... Almost without conscious thought, he found himself crossing the square, faster and faster, until he was bounding in the great thirty-foot strides the weak lunar gravity permitted.

There it was: Sam's rickety old raft. Dick jumped aboard, threw open the master valve. The jets blasted out flame; the raft rose sharply, straight up.

The square became small; Dick's radio hummed. Professor Dexter's voice came from the speaker. "Dick, you young fool, come back here; do you want to kill yourself?"

Dick made no answer. Somewhere, a hundred miles up in space above the moon, the *Australian Star* must pass. If he were lucky, he'd make contact and be taken aboard the ship. If he were not lucky—a new thought came to his mind: fuel!

He calculated, and a dull cold feeling came over him. He had filled the tanks before going out to Crazy Sam's cabin; the trip certainly had used a third, and possibly a half of the charge. With apprehensive eye he watched the needle on the fuel gauge drop, and measured against the rise of the altimeter needle, it moved alarmingly fast.

He looked over the side. The observatory was far below, a tiny spatter against the dark lip of the crater. The moonscape spread vastly to all sides; above swam the oyster-colored globe of Earth. Space opened all around, airless black nothingness, and Dick was alone.

Alone. The word had never had real meaning before. Into Dick's mind came an unwelcome memory: Henry's tale of the man who had gone adrift in his space-suit. Dick shuddered, hunched closer to the seat, as if it were warm. How easy, how ridiculously easy, to go mad — sheer awe, insignificance, aloneness. This was space-fear. Dick jerked his mind away, resolutely bent over the altimeter. The needle indicated a height of thirty miles, swinging rapidly as the raft gained speed. But the fuel needle was likewise swinging across its dial. Dick looked around the sky. The jets of the dispatch boat would be invisible in the wilderness of stars. No chance for help from Sende. He looked at his watch. Twenty minutes after seven. In another few minutes the *Australian Star* would sweep past, its course taking it over the observatory toward the old Security Station.

Dick glanced nervously from his watch to the altimeter. Not only must he rise to the correct altitude; he must also be sweeping at the same speed and in the same course as the spaceship. Otherwise it would whisk past with no chance for him to signal.

Seven-twenty-five, sixty miles high. Five minutes to rise forty miles. Dick felt a shadow begin to form over his mind. His bridges were burnt behind him now; if he missed the ship, he had insufficient fuel to lower himself once more to the moon. Well, there was no help for it; it was all or nothing. If he met the *Australian Star*, he, his father and the spaceship crew lived; if it passed him by — they all died.

He was almost to rendezvous altitude, with precious little fuel left. He pulled the joy stick back. Momentum would lift him to a hundred miles; now he needed forward speed to match the velocity of the spaceship.

He looked around the sky. Seven-twenty-nine, and the *Australian Star* might well be visible. The sky showed black — the deepest, most velvety black imaginable, and the stars shone bright as angry fireflies. But nowhere did he see the soft-gleaming metal shape, the band of windows shining like a necklace around the bow.

The minute hand on his watch drifted toward the bottom of the dial; the altimeter needle passed 97, then 98…Dick saw the *Australian Star* a trifle to his right, two miles above him, traveling fast.

The hull glinted in the Earthlight, the lights shone warm and friendly. It passed over him, sliding with a magnificent ease and detachment. Beside it coasted the dispatch boat, and now both ship and boat were over and gone — dwindling around the sky.

It was so fast that Dick had hardly time to realize what had occurred. The *Australian Star* was gone, beyond all hope of recall. His eyes dropped to the fuel gauge. The needle flickered close to the 'empty' mark. Certainly not enough to lower him again to the moon.

For at least a minute he sat stiff and rigid, his mind caught in a curious mood of incredulity. Unreal, the whole predicament. Unthinkable that the last moments of his life were ticking away; there must be a way by which he could save himself. His fingers opened and closed nervously inside his gauntlets... There had to be a way out! But what could it be? He could turn off the jets, let the gravity slow his upward momentum and drag him back toward the moon, to strike with the speed of a meteor. Or he could use what little fuel remained to attain an orbital speed, in which case he became a satellite of the moon: a human satellite circling the grim pockmarked globe forever and ever.

The first time around he might survive. But long before he had completed the second round he would be gasping for oxygen. Slowly he would smother inside his space-suit — and then, frozen and rigid, he would ride Crazy Sam's rocket-raft, around and around the moon, till the end of time.

# CHAPTER XIII

## *The Basilisk Strikes*

DICK SAT PARALYZED with indecision. It was clear that he was about to die. And never before had life seemed so wonderfully warm and colorful. Another idea came to sicken him: his father must die likewise, and the sacrifice which Dick was making was in vain. His eyes moistened; he thought of his mother on Venus. Twisting around on the raft, he looked over his shoulder to where Venus shone brightest among all the stars of the sky. He pictured his white home, the gigantic forests, the blazing flowers; never would he see them again.

He turned back to look along the course where the *Australian Star* had disappeared, with the wild fancy that he might hail the dispatch boat on the way back to the observatory. But no; the thought was a last groping at life. By now it would be far below him, skimming over the ghostly ruins of the old Security Station. And up here Dick drifted alone, gone from human knowledge. No one would ever see him again; no one would know where he had vanished. They would search the face of the moon, the dark crevasses, the weird shadows behind the craters; they would wander across Mare Baxteria and the Baxter Mountains, seek through the silver-fringed tumble of the lava sea. But never would they think to look high into the sky, where Dick would be drifting endlessly, set and rigid, a ghostly apparition which no human eye would ever see.

Dick's throat tightened, knotted; he looked around the sky. Was there no escape?

Earth above, dark moon below, wistful Venus behind, *Australian*

*Star* sliding on its course ahead...Behind, ahead, behind, ahead. The words rang in his head. A discrepancy: what was wrong?

His brain fumbled with an idea, twisting, lifting, kneading, as if it were a ball of dough. The idea suddenly took form: as clear and precise as if Dick had stepped from the dark into a bright room. Why had the *Australian Star* disappeared around the moon ahead when Venus lay behind?

There could only be one answer: it had to be that the *Australian Star's* course took it in an orbit entirely around the moon before it lined out for Venus.

Dick reacted not by thought, but as if instinct guided his hands. He swung the raft around, end for end, twisted the master valve hard over, pulled back two notches on the joy stick, aiming at a point in the sky a few degrees below Venus. Here, if his guess were correct, and if enough fuel remained in the tanks, the raft would intersect the course of the *Australian Star.*

Minutes passed; blue fire spat far down the sky below him. The fuel needle bounced back and forth against the stop. Dick sensed his speed increasing; the relative position of Moon, Earth and Venus underwent a subtle shifting. How much time would elapse before the *Australian Star* came into sight around the moon? He had no way of knowing, but it could not be long. The jets were failing — finally, irrevocably. The tongues of blue flame shortened, wavered. Desperately, Dick adjusted the trim of the raft, to drain the last ounces of hydrogen and oxygen into the outlets; the jets lengthened temporarily — blasted hard — and then went out.

The tanks were dry; the raft was a space-wandering hulk. Dick could only wait and drift — and hope.

The moon had become a globe; a cusp of the sun appeared on the serrated horizon like an orange showing past the edge of a circular saw. The light struck through Dick's helmet like bright flame. Hastily he swung up the metal screen and shielded his face...There — a movement! A glitter, a bright spark of reflection. He looked. A spaceship...It must be the *Australian Star!*

Now or never. Dick switched on his helmet radio, called in a husky voice. "*Australian Star!* Pick me up!" Leaning unconsciously forward, he watched the progress of the metal hull. It grew larger; it would pass close by. He rose to his feet, waved. "*Australian Star*! Help! Pick me up." Illogically he raised his voice, shouted. "*Australian Star*! Stop! Pick me up!"

A click sounded in his helmet — the most welcome sound Dick could ever hope to hear. "Who's calling? Where are you?"

Dick's throat swelled with uncontrollable emotion; he could hardly speak. "Where are you?" came the voice again, sharply.

"I'm on a raft, just ahead of you, toward Earth," Dick managed to gasp.

After a pause, the voice said, "We've got you on our radar... How do you happen to be out here on a raft?"

"It's a long story," said Dick. "It's got to do with pirates, the Basilisk."

"Oh," said the voice from the speaker. "Pirates, eh?" The tone was rather strange. Dick stared at the approaching hull. It showed the same silhouette as the *African Star* and the *American Star*, sister ships to the *Australian Star*; it had to be the *Australian Star*. Nevertheless, his voice trembled when he spoke. "Is my father aboard?"

There was no answer. The spaceship had passed across his course, but was evidently decelerating.

The voice spoke. "Alter your course to approach us."

Dick said, "I can't; I'm out of fuel; I'm just drifting."

"Stand by. We'll send out a boat."

Weakly, Dick sat down on the bench. Reaction was setting in; his legs felt numb and limp; a growing sense of detachment and unreality came over his mind.

The boat from the ship drew up alongside; a man in a space-suit rode the outside platform. Through the helmet Dick saw a round, heavy face, black bristling eyebrows. "Here," he said, "make fast the rope." He tossed a coil of line to Dick, who caught it, made it fast around the bench.

As they drew close to the spaceship, a detail which Dick had never noticed on the *African Star* caught his eye: a black opening just under the control dome from which protruded a heavy metal tube of ominous appearance. He had little time to look; a moment later the raft was jerked to the air lock and Dick stepped off, and into the spaceship. The outer door thudded shut behind him.

Through the porthole he saw several men: the first an enormous red-faced, red-haired man with nose no larger than the end of Dick's thumb; the second thin, dark and smiling. The third—Dick's heart leaped, melted into pure joy. The third was his father.

The inner door opened; Dick stumbled into the ship. His father ran forward; his face was deeply lined, older, more haggard than Dick had ever remembered.

He helped Dick out of the space-suit. "What in the world is the reason for all this, Dick?"

Dick took a deep breath. "We've got to turn back. The Basilisk is planning to attack!"

The great red-haired man pursed his mouth into a knot. "More of this nonsense about pirates."

"This is Captain Jugg, Dick," said Dr. Murdock. And he added wryly, "He doesn't believe that the pirates exist."

"But it's true!" cried Dick. "They lured you aboard this ship on purpose!" He blurted out the entire story.

His father listened without a word; Captain Jugg was clearly unimpressed. "Even if there were pirates," he said, "we got those bow-guns aboard. Useless iron they are, dead weight to cut down the payload, but we got 'em, and we've got men aboard who know how to use 'em."

"But the Basilisk certainly has more guns than you have," protested Dick.

"Balderdash," boomed Jugg. "Those other ships ran into meteors. There's no more pirates than there is space dragons. 'Basilisk'—hah!" He laughed contemptuously. "That's a tale to scare kids with." He turned to the small dark man. "Full speed ahead, Calkins; give her one full gravity till we're back on schedule."

Dr. Murdock looked an instant into Dick's face. "Are you—sure, Dick, about Mother?"

"I'm as sure as it's possible to be!" cried Dick. "Don't you see, the whole idea was to get you aboard this ship?"

Dr. Murdock was silent a moment, then turned to Captain Jugg, who stood off to the side. "Captain, I think we'd better put about and return to the moon."

"What?" bellowed Jugg. "Are you taken in by these fairy tales? I thought you were supposed to be a scientist, and know facts!"

"That's exactly correct," said Dr. Murdock dryly. "And the facts are as you heard them from Dick."

"The boy's been dreaming. All this talk about code messages — that's hundreds of years out of date."

"If Dick said he heard the message, he heard it," Dr. Murdock said coldly. "I trust Dick's observation completely."

Dick had been hopping from one foot to the other. "We've got to hurry, Captain Jugg."

"And now it's hurry, is it?" roared Jugg. "I'll have you know, young fellow, there's only one captain aboard the *Australian Star*, and that's me."

"But the Basilisk doesn't have your course; he just knows you're leaving the moon for Venus at a certain time, and that means he's got to attack early or else take the risk of losing you!"

"Dick, my boy," said Captain Jugg, "you get some rest. You need it. I don't see how you made it out here on that ramshackle old raft —"

Dr. Murdock shook his head grimly, put his arm around Dick's shoulder.

"— but it's taken a lot out of you. We've got a nice relaxing voyage ahead of us, and you'll be right as rain in a week or so."

Dr. Murdock spoke in a harsh voice: "Captain Jugg, I insist that you put about. You possibly are willing to risk —"

Jugg took a step forward. His legs were thick and heavy, the same width from thigh to ankle like the legs of an elephant. "Look here, Doc," he said roughly, his tiny nose twitching, "there's one thing I don't stand for, and that's passengers telling me how to run my ship!"

Calkins, the dark mate, slipped down from the bridge. "Ship's on steady one gravity, sir; I'm stepping down to check boat stowage."

Captain Jugg ignored him. "I've traveled space, man and boy, for thirty years, and I ain't gonna be told my business now by some over-educated eye doctor!"

Dr. Murdock stood back, his eyes glittering; Dick thought that never had he seen his father so angry. With tremendous effort he choked back his wrath and said in a strained voice, "I realize, Captain Jugg, that this is a very unusual request, and under ordinary circumstances I would not expect you to pay any heed to a passenger who asked you to change course —"

"Doc, you can talk till you're blue in the face —"

"—but let me put the facts in front of you. As my son told you, we have very little time —"

"Doc, I got work to do."

Dick went to the port, looked around the sky: stars, the great globe of Earth, the darkling bulk of the moon. He turned. His father and Captain Jugg were still arguing, and Captain Jugg was clearly enjoying the use of his authority.

Dick went quietly to the door, closed it, pulled down the heavy bolt. Captain Jugg and his father were locked away from the rest of the ship.

He raced up the spiral staircase into the bridge, which as he expected was temporarily deserted. He slammed the door, turned the key.

The controls were the same as those aboard the *African Star*. There — the repeater to the engine room; there — the automatic pilot, now aimed at Venus. He switched off the automatic pilot, seized the control knobs, twisted. The orientation sphere which showed the ship's direction in space slowly turned. Through the window Dick saw the Sun, Earth, Moon sweep across the sky. With the ship still turning he reached, jerked down the repeater, from single-gravity acceleration to two and a half gravities.

The sudden added weight pressed him to the deck; his muscles, accustomed to weak lunar gravity, quivered. Somewhere below he felt a jar, heard an angry shout.

Dick grinned. If the Basilisk attacked them now, at least he had done everything he possibly could.

The ship was still turning on its axis — fifty degrees — sixty — seventy — eighty — ninety. Now two and a half gravities were accelerating them at right angles to their former course. Dick let the nose of the ship swing still further, aimed it almost back toward the moon. There was an angry pounding on the door. "Open up in there!" came Captain Jugg's voice in a bull-like roar. "Open this door!"

Dick said nothing.

"Open up, or I'll break in!" The door rattled furiously.

Dick thought, go ahead, break it down; it's your own door.

Grunting and mumbling, Captain Jugg banged at the door.

The frail metal bent and strained. The sound ceased. Dick heard Captain Jugg panting; the more than double gravity was a great hardship. "When I lay my hands on you, you young scoundrel —" his threats died off in a spasm of cursing, and he renewed his attack.

The lock burst, the door flew open. Framed for an instant was the great red shape of Captain Jugg, with Calkins the mate smiling expectantly at his back. Then Captain Jugg lumbered forward. "You'll go to jail for this, you young criminal." He swung his great arms. Dick ducked, backed away from the controls.

"I'll take care of you later," grunted Jugg. He jerked up the repeater, back to single gravity; a moment later normal weight returned to them. "Now —" he twisted the control knobs "— it's back on course, and then you make the rest of the trip in irons."

"Captain," said Calkins in a strange, breathless voice.

"Well, what do you want?"

"Look."

Captain Jugg twisted, stared at the radar screen, slowly crossed the bridge. "Two ships, crossing our bow." He ran to the rack, took his binoculars, scrutinized space. "Two ships," he muttered. "I see 'em plain. What are they doing out here?"

"What do they look like, Captain?" said Calkins.

"Sisters to this one."

"The *Canopus* — the *Capella*," said Calkins under his breath.

"Looks like they were on our course, right enough," said Captain Jugg in a subdued voice. "Now they're sliding past — but they seem to be putting about." He gave a sudden froglike hop to the repeater, yanked it to three gravities.

Staggering under the tremendous acceleration, he made for the wall telephone. He bellowed, "Sparks, send out an SOS! It's pirates! Lucky I saw 'em in time."

Dr. Murdock came staggering into the bridge. He laughed harshly. "You mean it's lucky that Dick had enterprise enough to lock you up and take matters into his own hands!"

"Don't crow," muttered Jugg, watching the radar screen.

Dr. Murdock had only just started. Dick had never seen him so angry. His voice rang like a bell. "In my opinion you're not fit to be trusted with a spaceship. And as soon as I have the chance, I'll make my opinion known where it will do the most good!"

Jugg's face was red as raw beef. "If those are pirates, as you seem to think, you'll never have the chance to squeal. Because they're coming around as fast as they can come."

# CHAPTER XIV

## Crazy Sam's Notebook

DICK WENT TO THE WINDOW, looked through Jugg's binoculars. He saw two great ships studded with gun ports slewing sideways through space in an angry attempt to come about. "Looks like we've got a race on our hands," said Calkins, grinning his inane grin.

Dick said rather shortly, "If we lose — we lose our lives." He put the binoculars down; the effort of holding them to his eyes under three gravities made his arms ache. His father had gone to the door. "Come, Dick, we're in the way here; let's go below."

Cautiously and with great effort they descended the stairs. "Be very careful," Dr. Murdock warned. "We're under three gravities. A fall of six feet could kill you, just like a fall of eighteen feet at home." They staggered to the lounge on aching legs, sank with relief into a pair of soft chairs. Dick asked in a troubled voice, "Do you think they'll catch us?"

Dr. Murdock shook his head. "No. We got too much of a head start on them, and as soon as they hear us sending out emergency calls, they'll make themselves scarce." He looked at Dick speculatively. "Now, young man, I suppose I should thank you for risking your neck to save me, but I also should thrash you to an inch of your life for taking such terrible chances."

Dick grinned uncomfortably. "It turned out well — if the pirates don't catch up with us."

"It did this time, but it might not the next."

Dick remembered the awful hopelessness he had felt aboard the drifting rocket-raft, and shuddered.

"Now," said his father, "suppose you tell me the entire story."

Dick talked for fifteen minutes. When he had finished, his father sat a long moment looking off into space. "It's utterly certain," he said slowly, "that someone at the observatory is a traitor. But who? Who?"

Dick shrugged. "I have suspicions."

His father surveyed him dubiously. "Suspicions aren't much good, but let's hear them."

Dick hesitantly communicated his vague surmises. His father frowned doubtfully. "You can't convict or even accuse a man of criminal activity just because he looks peculiar; otherwise, three-quarters of us would be in jail."

The weight of acceleration lifted, giving way to a feeling of dizzying lightness. A moment later Calkins looked into the lounge.

"Captain Jugg's called down to the observatory for the dispatch boat; he's going to put you off at the moon."

Dr. Murdock rose to his feet. "Have we shaken off the pirates?"

"Yep, they gave up about ten minutes ago, took off back toward the Graveyard."

Dr. Murdock sighed. "That's a relief. Maybe I'll live to see my grandchildren after all." He looked sternly at Dick. "But I won't unless you take a few more pains to keep yourself alive than you have been taking."

Dick hung his head a little sheepishly.

"Incidentally," said his father, "I took your purple crystal to a jeweler for valuation. He says it's no doubt very valuable, but he could give me no exact figure because the gem is entirely unique. He'll sell it for you on commission and deposit whatever it brings to your account."

Dick nodded without great interest. At this moment money seemed of small importance.

An hour and a half later Sende met them in the dispatch boat. Crazy Sam's rocket-raft was lashed to the outside platform; without incident they returned to the observatory.

Dick took to bed and almost slept the clock around. He awoke with muscles still aching from the strain of the triple gravity. He took a shower, languidly dressed. As he was about to start downstairs his father looked in through the door. "I thought you'd never come to life… How do you feel?"

Dick yawned. "All in."

Dr. Murdock laughed. "A good breakfast will fix you up good as new."

They started downstairs. Dr. Murdock said, "I've interviewed almost everybody around the observatory. Naturally enough, no one admits to sending code messages, and no one knows anything about locking you in the library. Bayer was rather upset about the damage to his cabinets."

"Yes," said Dick, "I know. He yelled bloody murder when he opened the door and looked in."

Dr. Murdock restrained a grin. "Well, that's all in the past, and I hope it stays in the past. I don't care for any more excitement; it's giving me gray hairs. The government finally seems to be rousing itself; Captain Franchetti is coming out again today and I understand he's bringing official UN investigators."

Dick groaned. "I'll have to go through all that story again."

"Probably two or three times." Dr. Murdock gave him a hard look. "It's no more than you deserve for letting that curiosity bump get out of hand. Come on now; we'll see what Doc Mole's got for your breakfast."

The interrogation by the UN investigators more than lived up to Dick's expectations. There were three in all, one of whom unobtrusively manipulated the controls of a tape recorder.

They were particularly interested in the radio messages which Dick had intercepted, and took him over his story three different times. "Can't you check on these messages for yourself?" Dick asked finally.

"How do you mean?"

"Aren't all trans-space messages recorded at the monitor stations on the artificial satellites around Earth?"

"They are indeed — and that's why we're interested in these particular messages, because they were never picked up."

Dick blinked in perplexity. "That's strange."

"Very strange indeed." And the investigator fixed Dick with a glance that Dick considered unnecessarily penetrating.

Dick said stiffly, "Naturally I can't prove that I received the messages. And I suppose that since you can't find a record of them you suspect me of being —"

The investigator laughed. "No, Dick, I don't think that you're the Basilisk. I just want to make sure that your, well, imagination isn't running away with you."

"It isn't," said Dick shortly.

"Who do you think sent the message?"

"I haven't any idea. At least, I haven't any reason for my suspicions. They're just — suspicions."

"Let's hear them anyway."

Dick paused; when it came to point of fact, his speculations seemed built on the flimsiest structure imaginable. He said hurriedly, "They're just hunches, not even worth talking about. I haven't a fact in the world to back them up."

The investigator nodded. "We have hunches ourselves once in a while. We usually find that underlying the hunch is a solid knob of circumstance. Naturally we don't suspect a man of murder just because he looks like a movie criminal; all of us know better than that. Looks are for the most part very deceiving. However, sometimes a criminal reveals himself in subtle ways — a reaction to a word, calmness when excitement would seem more normal, small things which are still revealing. Do you understand?"

Dick nodded.

"I want you to go off by yourself and think. Try to identify the facts behind your hunches. They may or may not come to the surface. If they do, I want you to come back to me and report. Understand?"

Dick nodded. "I'll do my best. But I don't think I'll locate anything."

"Good. That's all for now then."

Dick left the lounge where the interview had taken place, wandered through the tubes linking the component buildings of the observatory. In the mess hall he met Hutchings.

Hutchings, who had been unsuccessfully trying to scrounge a piece of pie from Doc Mole, was in worse temper than usual. "Quite the hero now, aren't you?" he muttered from the corner of his mouth. "Well, don't try any fancy airs around me, Dick my boy, or I'll see that you regret it." He lit a cigarette, blew a cloud of ill-smelling smoke into Dick's face, snapped the match between his fingers, tossed it contemptuously over his shoulder. As luck would have it, Doc Mole happened to be watching from the galley. He roared in rage, came charging out with a meat cleaver.

Hutchings quailed against the dish cabinet. "What's the trouble?" he quavered.

Doc Mole pointed a quivering finger to a sugar jar. "Since when do you go throwing your nasty cigarette butts into my clean sugar, you sorry young whelp?"

"I didn't throw any cigarette butts," cried Hutchings; "it was only a match."

"*Only* a match, you say! *Only* a match! What's the idea throwing a match? Do you think I put out sugar bowls to catch your filth?" He raised the cleaver threateningly.

Hutchings ducked. "I'll take it out."

"Be quick about it or I'll give you the closest haircut you've ever had!"

Hutchings gingerly scooped the match from the sugar, carried it to an ash tray. "Now be off with you," roared Doc Mole, "and if you want to eat, you better not play a trick like that again."

Hutchings slunk off down the tube. Doc Mole nodded at Dick. "Nice day," he said mildly, and ducked back into his galley.

Dick automatically glanced outside at the changeless black sky, the million unwinking stars. One of Doc Mole's jokes. He drew himself a cup of coffee from the urn that was always kept full, took a seat, sat sipping and thinking…Strange that the code messages had not been monitored at the Earth stations — strange and possibly significant. Why should the code messages behave differently from any other messages leaving the observatory? Where did the shut-off occur? He knew that messages from the observatory were carried by automatic relay stations to the Security Station and there broadcast to Earth. If the code messages had left the Station transmitter, they must certainly have been recorded by one of the monitors on the artificial satellites.

Dick considered the implications. A remarkable conclusion thrust itself forward. It seemed as if the code messages went as far as the Security Station and no farther; which argued that the pirates were using the Security Station as a base! This conclusion, however, was challenged by other facts. How could Crazy Sam have been kept ignorant? Crazy Sam had been the caretaker, and although cantankerous, closemouthed and fanciful, he was the last person in the world Dick would have associated with pillage and murder.

On the other hand, the old Station was convenient to the trade lanes and close by the Graveyard. The underground hangars would afford a convenient hiding place for the captured spaceships; the loot could be stored in the warehouses until trans-shipment to anonymous dealers of Earth could be arranged.

Dick jumped to his feet, ran back to the lounge. But the investigators were in earnest conversation with Professor Dexter, who was shaking his head repeatedly, as if rejecting an idea proposed by one of the investigators. Dick hesitated a moment. They must certainly appreciate the significance of radio messages which went no farther than the Security Station; they probably would not thank him for bursting in with the obvious. He turned away; and many times in the future he was to wish that he had so burst in, pounded on the table to get attention, if necessary. But the future was hidden, and Dick passed quietly through the lounge, climbed the stairs to the library.

Isel Bayer raised his head, and the luxuriant white floss of his hair waved and rippled. The dark glasses shone challengingly toward Dick. "Back for more jackanape tricks?"

"No, Professor Bayer," said Dick politely. "I tried to explain to you that I'm very sorry for all the damage I caused."

Bayer nodded sourly. "Apologies don't repair damage. These books are too valuable to be risked with children; I'm afraid I'm going to have to ask you to —"

"I'm hardly a child," said Dick, cut to the quick, but still resolved to be polite. "And I'm certain nothing will ever happen like that again."

"I should hope not." Isel Bayer half turned away.

Dick, taking the silence for grudging toleration of his presence, passed quietly in and scanned the shelves.

The reflections on Isel Bayer's dark glasses followed him, but Dick could not be certain whether the eyes behind the glasses moved or not.

Presently he found the book he sought: *A History of Lunar Exploration and Development,* by Clarence Earl Sears. He thumbed quickly through the familiar chapters: the landings of the first chemically-powered ships; the first camps; the development of atomic power to space travel; the subsequent ten-year period when the more accessible ore deposits were exploited; the decline of operations due to overhead expense; and the chapter devoted to the Security Station.

Dick settled himself and began to read. He glanced down the pages rapidly. The names of the great lunar engineers jumped out of the print: Wainwright, Farrell, Boarman. He skimmed over statistics: so many tons of cement imported from Earth to be mixed with lunar gravel and thawed ice; so many tons of iron; so many square feet of resisto-glass; so many thousand gallons of airproofing paint to fill up the pores in the concrete.

He flipped rapidly through pages describing the political effects of the Security Station, the relaxing of vigilance, the final abandonment.

In growing disappointment he turned through the remainder of the book, but nowhere did he find a map of the Station itself.

He replaced the volume on the shelf, sought further. At last, tucked in an obscure corner, he discovered a little pamphlet entitled *The Greatest Fort of History,* by Thomas Guy Hand. Inside the title page was a folded map.

Dick eagerly laid it open on the table, studied the intricate arrangement of halls, hangars, warehouses, barracks, control offices. The Station spread out in a great *L*, with one leg sheltered under the rock wall of the nearby crater.

Into Dick's mind came a picture of another map he had seen — Crazy Sam's chart of the 'Baxter Caves'. There had been red and blue scrawlings across a neat outline identical to the one before him.

Dick looked over his shoulder to see Isel Bayer standing six feet behind him, his face expressionless.

Dick folded the chart with shaking fingers, returned the book to its place, left without a word.

He went to his room, flung himself on his bed. Now more than ever did he want that chart. It was not in Crazy Sam's hut. And Dick, remembering the crude picture of the thing with the golden eyes, felt little cold whispers coursing along his skin.

Was the golden-eyed creature indeed the Basilisk? Did he have his headquarters under the old Security Station?

Dick rose to his feet, went to the window. If he had Crazy Sam's chart, many of these questions might be resolved. The chart had not been in Sam's hut, on his body or on Bronco Bert the rocket-raft.

Where could it be? One possibility remained — the dark floor of Baxter's Bottomless Pit.

# CHAPTER XV

## Flood of Fire

DICK STARED ACROSS THE MOONSCAPE with unseeing eyes. In his mind was the picture of Crazy Sam's death: the great boulder, Sam's reeling body and contorted face. Once again he heard the cries ringing in through his helmet radio. Dick gritted his teeth. He must fly out to the Bottomless Pit; he must lower himself once more into the chasm. Dangerous, and yet he must go, secretly and alone. Even to tell his father was to risk passing the news on to the seemingly more-than-human presence of the Basilisk. Likewise, it was more than probable that his father would forbid him to make the trip.

Dick moved with feverish haste, keeping doubts and second thoughts to the back of his mind. He ran downstairs, quietly passed through the lounge into the ward room where he slipped into his spacesuit, clamping on a fresh tank of oxygen.

Three minutes later he was outside in the square. The edge of the rising sun cast long black shadows; dodging through these, Dick made his way to where Crazy Sam's rocket-raft had been dropped.

The first necessity was fuel; the raft was still empty after Dick's epic flight. He measured the distance to the pumps with his eye: a hundred feet. Either the raft had to be brought to the fuel or the fuel to the raft. Dick decided that the first would be simpler, since to obtain a container and a funnel he would have to go to Lobscombe, and this he had no wish to do.

He looked at the raft. On Earth it might have weighed three or four hundred pounds; here on the moon it would weigh hardly fifty. Dick stepped through the frame, and grasping the struts to either side, lifted it to the level of his waist. The raft made an awkward load; Dick was glad to set it down beside the pump.

He moved with haste. Lobscombe might or might not object to Dick helping himself to fuel; the best way to avoid the issue was to avoid Lobscombe.

Dick was in luck; three minutes later the two tanks were full of the liquid gas. As he hung up the flexible metal tube he glanced across the square to the administration building. A figure standing by the window moved back out of sight.

Dick stared, his heart beating. Someone had been watching him, someone whose sense of guilt had made him furtive. If there had not been that involuntary start, Dick would have thought nothing of the matter. But furtive motion there had been, and no one at the observatory would be furtive except one person — the murderer, the traitor, the Basilisk spy.

Dick hesitated, half his heart for the adventure gone. Still, if he jumped on the raft, took off, he could be far out and lost among the crazy shadows of lunar morning before his enemy could follow. He hesitated no longer. He seated himself, opened the master valve. The rocket-raft jerked alive, rose from the ground in the now familiar series of dives and swoops.

Dick adjusted the flow to the four jets; the raft steadied. He opened wide the master valve, hauled back the joy stick; the raft plunged up and away from the observatory. Looking over his shoulder he fancied he saw movement in the square, but the harsh blacks and dazzling whites confused his eyes and he could not be sure.

Now he rode in the full glare of the sunlight. Below him each crater, each hump, crag, jut and spine cast a shadow fifty times its own height. To his right spread the tortured expanse of Lake Baxter; to his left, a gigantic black palisade reared two miles up from a plain of pumice.

Dick looked behind. The observatory was a toy village, each detail brilliant, sharp, distinct across the vacuum. There was a sudden empty feeling in his stomach; a dark spot rising from the square? He stared, but could not be sure. Best not to take chances; he knew that his life depended on his own craft.

He cut the jets almost off, fell toward the moon. Only a few hundred yards from the surface he pushed the joy stick hard over, turned up the power, skidded like a water-skipper low over the ground. In the shadow of the great palisade he landed, watched the sky.

Ten minutes passed without incident. Dick, reassured, reached for the master valve then paused, struck by a new thought. If someone wished to follow him, surely they would not rely on sight alone. They would have — he jumped to the ground, gave the raft a careful inspection.

Tacked under the seat he found an inconspicuous little tattletale radio cell, no larger than a pocket watch. Almost certainly it was broadcasting a steady set of signals; almost certainly his enemy was quietly approaching, following the beam.

Dick grinned. Two could play the game. He pried off the cell, dropped it into a black hole which gaped a few yards away. Jumping on his raft, he rose quickly to a ledge up the face of the palisade. He landed in the shadow at the back of the ledge, alighted, settled himself where he could watch unseen.

Time passed with hypnotic sluggishness. The sun inched up over the horizon slow as a snail, twenty-eight times as slow as an Earthly sunrise. The moonscape stretched before Dick's eyes, an airless desolate desert.

Sliding low over the ground came a small raft. Dick stiffened, strained his eyes. It was clearly one of the observatory rafts; a man in a hooded space-suit rode the seat. He came in such a way as to avoid being seen, dodging into the shadows, slipping low through declivities and depressions. Cautiously he slid his raft toward the base of the palisade.

Dick leaned forward, craning his neck. The raft was almost below him. It stopped; the man aboard seemed puzzled. He carefully scanned the rock along the base of the palisade, inspected the pumice plain. He stepped off the raft. Try as Dick might, he was unable to see the face inside the helmet. The man saw the pit; he stopped short, then advanced slowly.

Dick rose to his feet, picked up a jagged chunk of rock three feet in diameter. He carried it to the lip of the palisade, paused, gauged his distance, dropped it.

The boulder fell gently at first, picked up speed, struck the raft with shattering force. Dick saw the rear jet break loose, saw oxygen and hydrogen spill across the rocks.

Sound did not carry across the vacuum, but the man felt the shock. He whirled, gazed in consternation at the broken raft. He glanced up, his eyes met Dick's: baleful yellow eyes.

Dick backed away, hastily boarded his raft. A moment later he was skidding at full speed toward Baxter Point.

He looked over his shoulder. Who was the man in the space-suit? Dick knew of only one man with lion-yellow eyes: A. B. Sende. When he returned to the observatory it would be easy enough to make sure. And after the man's identity had been established it would be simple enough to send out a search party to pick him up. Of course — and Dick looked back toward the observatory, still visible — it was possible to move very swiftly across the moon, especially across a smooth pumice plain. The man, Sende or not, might well return to the observatory on foot.

He must hurry. He opened the master valve to its widest extent. Blue flame lanced astern, the raft fled like a frightened bird across the nightmare landscape.

Ahead rose Baxter Mesa. Dick guided the raft down toward the precarious ledge. He took one last look around the sky, dropped into the black chasm that was Baxter's Bottomless Pit. The rock walls rose past him; the avenue of stars above grew narrower and narrower. Down, down, down, with every muscle tense, blue flame lighting the walls with eery glow.

Down, ever farther into the hidden parts of the moon. The street of stars became a far path, a line. The walls which no eye but his own had seen towered past, closing in ever closer, and at last the bottom.

Dick landed, briskly jumped off the raft. He flicked on his dome searchlight. Where had Sam struck? It must be nearby. He started off along the narrow floor of the crevasse, went fifty feet, a hundred feet. Something glimmered ahead. Dick rushed forward eagerly. He bent, picked it up: Sam's pouch. Inside was the notebook.

Dick opened the book; the red and blue network over the neat black L appeared. Satisfied, he tucked it into his own pouch, turned back toward the raft. He climbed aboard, started the jets. The rock walls slid down past him, faster and faster as the narrow gap far above became a trickle of stars, a path, a street, a broad expanse — and Dick was out in free space.

He rose high; Baxter's Bottomless Pit became a split in ancient stone, Baxter Mesa a trestle. He slid over the Sam Baxter Range, crossed Mare Baxteria. Somewhere below him — Dick chuckled — someone was furiously plodding the weary miles back to the observatory.

Dick landed in the square, jumped off, ran toward the administration building. He entered through the air lock, slipped out of his space-suit. Now to find his father. Dick felt a qualm of uneasiness. Even though he had Crazy Sam's chart in his pocket, his father would not think too well of his exploit, especially when he learned of the still-anonymous man who must now be close to the observatory.

The lounge was empty. Dick ran up to the second floor, looked into the bookkeeping office. Hutchings sat at his desk. "What do you want?" he growled.

"I'm looking for my father," said Dick. "Have you seen him?"

"No." Hutchings turned back to his work.

Dick went down the passage, knocked at Professor Dexter's dark-room. There was no answer, nor was Professor Dexter in his quarters. He continued to the library, opened the door, looked inside. Empty.

Dick ran upstairs, but the rooms he shared with his father were vacant.

Somewhat puzzled, he descended to the lounge, started through the tube. He knocked at the radio shack. No answer. In the mess hall he found Curtis, the chemist, drinking coffee. Curtis had just come in from the laboratory and had seen no one. "They're probably all up at the telescope," he said.

Dick ran to the ward room, jumped back into his space-suit, passed out the air lock into the square. In thirty-foot leaps he ran across the black glass of the crater floor, started up the slope. The telescope came into view, the tube lying almost horizontal. Dick paused in his stride, stared, and his heart stood still.

The tube was pointed directly at the sun; the sun-shield was swung back. The full glare of the sun, collected and concentrated by the mirror, poured in a terrible blazing flood into the observer's cage.

Who was inside? Dick shrieked out in sudden agony. He knew who was inside — his father.

# Chapter XVI

## *The Eyes of the Basilisk (I)*

FOR A TIME THAT PERHAPS could be measured in tenths of seconds Dick stood transfixed; and short though the time was, it seemed as if the whole of his life were passing. Later he never remembered his next actions. He must have run forward, torn frantically at the drive-switches in the platform control booth; when the tube swung to the landing stage he was there to pull open the door to the observer's cage.

Then a spectacle he would never forget as long as he lived: his father came staggering out, stary-eyed, his space-suit blistered and boiling, the helmet melted egg-shape. As he fell to the floor of the landing stage, a mirror clattered from his hands.

As Dick bent over him he went limp, his eyes closed, his mouth fell open. Dick cried out, but there was no answer, no sound. He lifted his father — easy in the weak gravity — carried him as swiftly as possible downhill.

The journey was a nightmare. His father's arms and legs sagged; his head lolled horribly. Dick was sure he was dead. Somehow or other he carried him through the air lock, into the lounge; suddenly the room was full of people.

A stern and white-faced Professor Dexter removed the helmet while Dr. Lister, the observatory medic, pulled away the suit. A stretcher was brought. Dr. Murdock, limp, breathing heavily, moaning a little, was carried upstairs to the infirmary.

Dick numbly removed his own space-suit, went slowly up to the infirmary, presently found courage enough to go in. Dr. Lister was spraying his father's face with some sort of balm.

"Is he — will he —"

Dr. Lister looked up. "Yes, he'll pull through. He's had a close call — heat exhaustion and burns. I'll keep him under sedation for a few days and then I think he'll be right as rain."

"Is there anything I can do?" asked Dick. "Does he need a blood transfusion or anything of that sort?"

Dr. Lister shook his head. "No, Dick. The best thing you can do is go to your room and rest. Here." He gave Dick two white tablets. "To quiet your nerves. The main thing is, don't worry. Your father had a very close call; another minute in that furnace would have done for him. But as it is, he'll be perfectly all right. Now you go and rest."

Dick turned away, listlessly wandered downstairs. People he hardly noticed asked him questions he answered automatically. There was much hushed conversation, many emphatic exclamations.

Dick's eyes, moving here and there, came to rest on a tall figure standing quietly in the doorway, a man with yellow eyes and a keen profile: Sende. Like a hammer blow the memory of the man whose raft he had wrecked and of whose identity he was still uncertain came to him.

He watched Sende as if to read the answer to his question in the yellow eyes. Sende stared back, and Dick thought he noticed a slight tightening of the knife-slit mouth. Then he was gone, and Dick was left looking at the empty doorway.

After a few moments he rose to his feet, went quickly to his room. He stood in the doorway a minute, then entered and locked the door.

He sat down at the desk, opened Crazy Sam's notebook. The chart of the Security Station with the red and blue scrawling stared up at him. What was here that Crazy Sam had considered so tremendously important? Dick turned the pages, frowning at Crazy Sam's barely decipherable handwriting. Odd snatches here and there he could read: ' — must have died slowly. The few remaining — ' ' — dangerous and difficult. Will never under any circumstances reveal — ' ' — this one has learned the language, and his purpose is to make the world once more a fit place — ' ' — never must I be surprised at his disguise, no matter where or when — '

Dick turned the pages and came to the chart. At the bottom of the page Sam had hurriedly scribbled a few words of explanation: 'Blue — level; red — slope; circles are opening to the surface; crosses are shutoffs when Station broke into and blocked off the passages.' Apparently the Baxter Caves were charted by the red and blue lines.

He read on with mounting excitement. 'Levels start with *A*.' Referring to the chart, Dick saw that the colored lines were peppered with letters of the alphabet.

He turned back to the legend. 'Lowest is the old town, at *R*. Undoubtedly caves go deeper, but I have been reluctant —'

Dick grimaced. If the caves were such as to daunt so solitary a man as Crazy Sam, what effect would they have on a normal person?

He scrutinized the chart for a moment, then turned the page. Here was more of Crazy Sam's scribbling, like a row of gnarled roots. Dick squinted, looked sideways. 'Opening No. 1 is by my hut; opening No. 2 is under biotite ledges —'

Dick turned back to the chart, found the circle with a '1' inside; here must be Crazy Sam's hut. From the No. 1 opening Dick traced a course toward the Security Station. With care and caution the Station could be approached and investigated by means of the underground passage.

Dick rose to his feet, walked back and forth in a torment of indecision. In whom could he confide? Somehow the news must be transmitted either to Commander Franchetti or the UN Bureau of Investigation. But how? Whom could he trust? Least of all Sende, the radio operator, who must handle the message. His father was unconscious; there was no one else at the observatory of whom Dick was completely sure. For all practical purposes he was alone. A new thought struck him. If as he suspected, it was Sende who had pursued him across the moon, who then had tried to kill his father in the telescope? Did the Basilisk have two agents at the observatory?

Dick lay down on the bed fully clothed. His muscles relaxed; he realized that he was terribly tired. Wearily he got to his feet, removed his clothes, and after some hesitation took one of the pills Dr. Lister had given him. Twenty minutes later he was asleep.

Immediately after awakening he visited the infirmary, to find that his father was still under sedation. He went to the mess hall and ate a thoughtful breakfast, then wandered restlessly through the various tubes and buildings of the observatory for half an hour.

Gradually he became aware of a peculiar tension among the observatory personnel: a muttering uneasiness which seemed to have no focus, no theme. It was as if a sense of imminence were building up, the heaviness which gathers in the air before a thunderstorm. Dick went to stare out across the square at Crazy Sam's old rocket-raft.

There was still fuel in the raft, sufficient to take him to the Station and back — should he choose to go. He gave it some thought. It would be dangerous, no question about it; the Basilisk would not blink twice at taking his life. There was always the possibility, of course, that the Security Station was bare and empty, but somehow Dick did not think this was the case.

Probably the Basilisk was ignorant of Crazy Sam's chart; certainly he was unaware that Dick now had it in his possession. In view of this fact there seemed no reason why Dick should not with perfect safety explore the Security Station. He thought fleetingly of his father; carefully he removed the thought and hid it at the back of his mind. His father certainly would not approve. Still, thought Dick, someone must investigate the Station; he was as able as anyone else. If he were caught — icy fingers clutched the pit of his stomach. But he would not be caught. He would approach Sam's hut by a roundabout route, making sure that no one followed him, that there was no tracer-cell fastened to the raft.

Excited now, he ran up to his room, where he disengaged the chart from Crazy Sam's notebook. He slung his camera around his neck, slipped downstairs to the ward room, where he climbed into his spacesuit. As an afterthought he clamped a spare bottle of oxygen into the harness and also an extra battery for his searchlight — precautions which he thought probably would be unnecessary, since he planned to be gone from the observatory only three or four hours at the most.

He passed outside through the air lock, ran in long bounds to the rocket-raft. He jumped aboard, reached for the master valve. A shadow fell across his helmet. Turning with a start of alarm, he looked into the piercing eyes of A. B. Sende.

"Going for a ride?" asked Sende in a carefully casual voice.

"I'm going prospecting," said Dick. "I'm going to look for some more tourmalines."

"It's a dangerous pastime, this rocket-rafting," said Sende, his metallic voice completely expressionless. "If I were you, I'd stay pretty close to home. In fact, I wouldn't go out at all. Peculiar things happen to rafts — and the people that ride them."

Dick turned the valve. "I plan to be very careful."

"Sometimes that isn't enough."

Dick made no answer. The jets spat flame, the raft rose into the black sky. Looking down he saw Sende standing quietly, watching him without expression.

Dick set out toward Baxter Mesa, skimming low over the lava ocean, now hot and dusty in the sunlight. He slipped into a little crater, inspected the raft: no radio tattletale. The sky behind seemed clear of pursuit. He rose once more into the air, flew out toward the Security Station, dodging among the jagged spires of a great mountain chain to confuse anyone who might be following.

At last confident that he came unfollowed, he alighted in a black little valley a hundred yards from Crazy Sam's hut. He watched a few moments; there was no light, no motion. The scene was as dead as only a moonscape can be.

The Security Station was invisible behind a razor-backed ridge. Dick was certain that his approach had not been observed; nevertheless he did not relax his caution. Keeping to the black shadows, he slipped across the rock to Sam's hut. He glanced in: peaceful, empty.

He drew the chart out of his pouch and examined it.

Opening No. 1 — near the hut. Two minutes later he found it, a fissure leading into the hill fifty feet distant.

Dick took a last look around the sky, switched on his searchlight, entered the fissure. The route he had traced for himself ran in a more or less direct line toward the Station. If Sam's chart were accurate, finding his way should be simple; it was merely a matter of continuing straight along the main tunnel, avoiding the two passages which opened to the right, the three to the left.

The passage showed the faintest possible signs of use: a few sharp corners chipped away, a gap broken in a dike which ran across the way.

The opening disappeared behind him; rock surrounded him entirely — glistening mica schist, glossy obsidian, dull basalt. Dick walked slowly, keeping a sharp watch to either side. It suddenly occurred to him that he was invading the region where, according to Sam, the lunar natives lived. Dick's step faltered. In his preoccupation with the Basilisk he had completely forgotten the creatures which Crazy Sam insisted still inhabited these caves.

Dick looked doubtfully around — up, down, back, forward. Suppose these natives really existed? It was clear that if they did exist, they wished to preserve the secret of their existence. And it was nearly certain that if they caught him they would deal harshly with him. But the question remained — did they exist? It seemed logically improbable — from where would they derive the energy necessary for life? How could they survive in the absolute cold, in the dark airless passages? On the other hand, Dick knew that the more men learned about space and the outer regions, the fewer things it became safe to speak of as impossible. Suppose that traces of the ancient lunar atmosphere still lurked in these caves? Suppose radioactive minerals supplied warmth?

Dick shrugged, stepped forward. If the natives were real, he must be wary of them as well as of the pirates. Certainly this particular passage was dead, airless, cold. If they required air and warmth, he would not find them here.

He came to a halt, snapped off his light, peered ahead for a possible glimmer of light. But before his eyes adjusted to the darkness, nerves got the better of him; shakily he reached up, switched the light back on. Standing alone in the blackness, where strange unhuman creatures might or might not exist, was by no means a relaxing exercise.

Sweating now, darting glances to right and left, Dick continued along the tunnel. He passed the first opening Sam had indicated on his map; so far, so good. A hundred feet farther he came to the second. Correct and in accord with the map.

He went on slowly, his dome light creating a small living cell of light in the dead lunar artery. At the third side opening he mustered up his courage, switched off the light, and forced himself to stand perfectly quiet while he counted to a hundred.

His eyes still saw only blackness — so deep and heavy that it possessed its own mass and density. He switched on the light; the radiance pressed back the clotted dark.

Dick went forward. Rock, shadow, light. Darkness before, darkness behind. Twice he passed side openings, twice he extinguished his light and waited in the darkness. Under his feet he felt softness; looking down, he saw a spongelike bed of pumice. Down the center of the passage it was crushed and broken; and here — Dick looked closely — here was the clear imprint of a foot. It was a regulation space boot, rather small, fitted with cleats; evidently Crazy Sam's track. Somewhat reassured, Dick continued.

He passed the fifth side opening; now he must be close to the Station. He turned off his light once again. Ahead — the hint of a glimmer? Dick stared, cautiously advanced through the dark. The light became stronger. Presently he made out its source: a small square of glass set into the wall. He peered through and found himself looking into a rather large room, cluttered with broken crates and boxes. Aside from the debris the room held nothing of interest; Dick, however, felt a thrill of excitement. Light meant habitancy; there was almost no doubt remaining that the old Station was being used for illicit purposes.

It occurred to Dick to wonder how the pirates had persuaded Sam to secrecy. Queer and crotchety as he had been, Sam had certainly been honest. How had they sealed his mouth?

Dick turned on his dome light, continued down the passage. Sam's tracks in the pumice became clearer and fewer. Evidently he had come this way only two or three times.

The passage took a sudden turn, rose abruptly. Dick scrambled up the slope, came to a frozen halt. There had been nothing to see but light and shadow, darkness and rock; now all at once there was too much.

A broad band of glass extended across the wall. Through this glass poured a flood of light. Dick glanced warily up at the window, then returned to that which had caught his eyes at first: the footprints in the pumice. One set of these were clearly Crazy Sam Baxter's; the second set, which entered out of the darkness ahead, were very long and very narrow, with three peculiar indentations where human toes would be. The shape was like an exclamation mark with three dots below.

It was clear what had happened. Crazy Sam had been standing at the window, perhaps sketching. Something had come stalking out of the darkness; Sam had whirled in his tracks. The two had stood face to face, for how long the prints gave no hint. Then Sam had turned and gone his way, and likewise the thing with the golden eyes.

Dick's skin crawled along his neck, the same spot where a dog's hackles rise. He looked up at the band of glass, took a step forward, paused, his heart thudding with an emotion he had never felt before. It was fear — a strange kind of fear that had the effect of numbing his knees and drying his mouth. Fear he had felt before, certainly, but never this fear of the unknown which almost reduced him to helplessness.

He forced his legs into motion, forced himself to stir. Step by step he approached the band of glass; bit by bit the scope of the great room beyond came into his range of vision. At last he stood gazing full through the window.

The walls were part concrete, part native rock; the floor seemed to be a kind of rubbery composition. At the far end was a low stage which gave the room the semblance of an auditorium. The main floor of the room held four rows of rude tables; at these tables sat a large number of men, eating voraciously from steaming bowls. Earthmen they definitely were, and Dick's breath came a little easier. Hard, mean, shifty-eyed ruffians; bloated and arrogant bullies; sly-eyed men who ate with one arm looped about their plates. Scarred, pulp-nosed, weasel-faced — the stench of evil came plainly through the glass to Dick's brain. All races, all nationalities were here; evil, like heroism and generosity, knows no boundary. But they were men. Pirates certainly, and hanging would be far too good for all of them — but human beings. Who then was the Basilisk? Why had —

There was motion at the side of the stage, a flutter of a black cloak. The men noticed, stiffened. Uneasiness rippled across the room, jaws champed slower on food, the whites of eyes showed nervously. Dick wondered what manner of man could instill such obvious terror in these creatures. Or was it a man?

Slowly it came out on the platform; the men at the benches froze, the spoons and forks dropped slowly to the table, every head followed the slow progress of the creature.

It seemed thin and somehow spidery, although a black cape enveloped most of the body. The feet, encased in black velvet slippers, were long and narrow, split at the front into three arched toes. A soft broadbrimmed black hat was pulled down upon the creature's head. The clothes were almost like those assumed by the spy in Victorian melodramas. But there was nothing Victorian about the face — and the face was for the most part eyes. Two great golden disks, radiant as sun-shot topaz, were these eyes. The centers were brilliant oily-black ovals, glittering with inhuman malignance.

Dick forced himself to raise his camera. The exposure, aperture and focus automatically adjusted themselves; he pressed the trigger.

When he looked down once more the Basilisk had raised his eyes, was staring straight into his — and the gaze froze his brain to cold jelly.

How had he been detected? In sudden anguish Dick remembered his dome light. He had not turned it off; when he looked across the auditorium, the glare had caught the Basilisk's eye as if Dick had waved a flag.

Dick sought to stir, to flee. But his legs felt as if they were a hundred miles away. Fascinated, he stared at the glowing golden eyes. A radiance from the Basilisk's brain reached across the distance, held him transfixed. He sensed motion among the pirates; a pair of them hurried out of the room. Dick whimpered like a puppy, tried to let his knees collapse. To no avail; the inhuman gaze held him like a pin through a butterfly. Under his feet Dick felt the vibration of heavy steps.

# Chapter XVII

## *Lost in the Lunar Caves*

Two bulky shapes entered the passage. Dick, unable to tear his gaze from the window, sensed them from the corner of his eyes. His feet rebelled against the paralysis of his brain; his knees tensed, thrust him headlong toward the opening of the passage. Will, muscular control came back to him; desperately he sought to avoid the dark forms.

He failed. One tackled him around the knees, the other deftly looped a rope around his neck. Ten seconds later Dick found himself being dragged unceremoniously down the passage. One man walked ahead, hauling on a rope to his neck; the other came behind, holding a similar rope taut. Dick's hands were free, but resistance was impossible; he could move neither forward nor backward except as the two ropes dictated. He was marched along the corridor like a pig to market.

The anger and confusion boiling in his mind began to give way to alarm. His captors made no sound; suddenly they stopped short, heaved up together on their ropes. Dick found himself neatly lifted, swung out over a dark opening, dropped.

He fell perhaps twenty feet; in the weak lunar gravity distances were hard to estimate. The light overhead was cut off; Dick rose to his feet, stood in total darkness. After a taut moment he switched on his headlamp; as he suspected, he was imprisoned in a kind of dungeon.

One wall was a flat vitreous surface, gleaming like a slab of new tar. The other three walls were native rock, the floor was gray concrete; the ceiling was rock with a steel hatch through which he had been dropped.

Dick pulled the rope loose from around his neck, feeling dismally lost and lonesome; every ounce of him yearning, wishing that he had remained at the observatory. What were the chances that the Basilisk would allow him to live? There were none. None whatever.

Dick peered at his oxygen gauge; this cell might easily be his execution chamber. The pirates had merely to ignore him until he breathed the last of his oxygen. They would not have long to wait. Four hours for the tank in use, six hours for his spare. Ten hours. Dick's knees felt watery; he leaned against the wall.

He walked around the cell. A few fragments of rotten pumice lay on the floor; otherwise it was empty. There was no scope for cleverness or trickery. In the course of his life he had read of a hundred marvellous escapes; but here, face to face with reality, escape was impossible. Clearly, obviously, completely impossible. Only when they opened the hatch and dragged his body out would he escape. Suppose…Dick's mind glowed like an ember in a sudden draft of air; he unclamped his spare tank of oxygen, hid it under the loose bits of pumice.

There was nothing to do now but wait. He seated himself gingerly on the floor. After a moment, he reached up, turned off his head lamp.

Time passed. Dick might have dozed. He awoke with a curious sense of urgency. He looked from side to side — the darkness was unrelieved. Beset by a rush of unreasoning fear, he raised his hand to light his search lamp, then paused.

Two spots of yellow light appeared on the glossy black wall. Dick watched in amazement. Insects? Electricity? He blinked. The spots of light were beyond the wall. He nervously switched on his dome lamp.

The lights disappeared; the shiny black wall confronted him. Dick uncertainly turned out the light; the spots of yellow glow reappeared. Now they were larger; they appeared to have small dark centers. Dick watched fascinated. The eyes of the Basilisk — behind the wall!

Paralysis once more began to steal over his muscles. With a tremendous effort Dick turned away his gaze; gritting his teeth, he fought the pressure of the great golden eyes. "It's in my mind," he whispered desperately. "It's hypnotism; it's because I'm afraid…He's not supernatural, only another live creature…"

Dick forced himself to look back to the glass wall; on the other side the golden eyes stared with the inhuman detachment of a fish looking through the side of an aquarium.

Dick stared back, clinging to his will with every shred of mental force at his command. He rose shakily to his feet; suddenly he knew that he had won, that the Basilisk had lost his power to freeze him with a glance. So far as it went, it was a victory.

The golden eyes hung steady, looking toward Dick with a dispassion far beyond malignance. Dick felt like a moth under the gaze of a spider.

Light began to fill the room behind the glass wall. The Basilisk made a subtly terrifying silhouette: low broad-brimmed black hat, the strange face, the gaunt frame hunched under the black cape.

The speaker inside of Dick's helmet clicked; in Dick's ear sounded a voice. "I wonder that I have allowed you to live as long as I have."

Dick made no answer. The voice was metallic and precise. Where had Dick heard such a voice before? He looked wonderingly into the golden eyes with the glittering black centers.

"You have disarranged my plans; you have come to spy on me; you have done more than any man living to injure and inconvenience me."

Dick asked huskily, "How do you know all this?"

The Basilisk ignored him. "I will gladly see you die. And after you, your father."

"But why?" Dick burst out, "Why do you want to harm my father? What has he done to you?"

"He stands in my way."

"So will any other Chief Astronomer. You'll have to kill them all, and you can't do it. Because sooner or later the Space Navy will hunt you down."

"The Space Navy is nothing. There is no navy in space except my own ships; I will allow no other." The Basilisk's voice became sharper, more metallic. "I have a secure base, the Lunar Observatory is mine. Earth ships fear to venture into my realm; already my power is felt. I shall master the outlying planets; there shall be a million corpses; a million slaves."

Dick began to perceive that, nonhuman or not, the brain which motivated the Basilisk was diseased.

"Already the plans are made," said the Basilisk. "Your body will hardly be cold before my ships set forth."

"Set forth for where?" Dick could not help asking.

"I ride to Mars, to Perseverine. I shall raze the city with fire, and kill, kill, kill…" His voice rose in pitch. "I gain all the wealth of the Martian metal works, all the production of the Martian machine shops!"

"But what good does it do you?" cried Dick. "You can't spend the money; the men and women have never injured you."

"They will know my power; they will acknowledge my will. First Perseverine, then all of Mars and all of Venus and then — who knows? Perhaps —" He stopped, leaned slightly forward, seemed to focus his golden eyes even more fixedly on Dick. "Inside your little inefficacious pulp of a brain you think the Basilisk is mad; he is crazy. I say to you, you do not know what sanity is. I am the Basilisk. In later days men will guide their ways by me, as the sun guides a billion clocks. Men shall say, 'Thus did the Basilisk; we will do likewise', and they shall be right. And they shall say, 'This was as it was done before, but the Basilisk has interposed, and now it is bad; now it is insane. Only the Basilisk is sane; only the Basilisk is the norm; only the Basilisk knows.'"

The voice had risen to a shrill yammer. Dick frowned. Where had he heard that voice? It was at once familiar and strange, as if well-known intonations had been passed through an electronic distortion apparatus. Dick frowned. Something was evading him, something of which he should be aware was passing him by.

"Now I leave you to die," came the Basilisk's voice. "You can count the hours of your life on the gauge of your oxygen tank; spend those hours wisely; you will never have others. Three times you have evaded my reach; now there is an end. So make your peace with the hereafter, because you will never leave this cell alive." The Basilisk rose to his feet, the lights dimmed, and blackness seeped back into the cell.

In nightmare fascination Dick watched the yellow eyes recede, becoming two yellow parentheses as the Basilisk turned his back, the bulging edges of the eyes showing past his head.

The eyes vanished; Dick was alone.

He moved restlessly back and forth across the cell, then caught himself up short. Motion consumed oxygen; he must move as little as possible, every breath was precious.

He stretched himself out near his spare tank of oxygen. This was his single hope for life — the possibility that the pirates would give him a reasonable time to smother, on the basis of his single tank, then come for his body. Once he was free of the dungeon, he once more had a chance to escape. No matter how slim a chance, it was a chance.

Dick lay still, breathing as shallowly as possible. Time inched past as if the seconds rode the backs of snails. He thought of his home on Venus, his mother, his sister, the voyage across space aboard the *African Star*, his life at the observatory. He thought of his father, he thought of the Basilisk. Deep in his mind something stirred, something he could not remember. He remembered his camera; there was one exposure in its catch box. The single existing photograph of the Basilisk.

Time moved on, deliberate as a glacier. Three times he switched on his dome light, looked at his oxygen gauge; remorselessly the needle fell; remorselessly the sands of his life ran out … For it was entirely possible — in fact probable — that the pirates would not think to drag up his body before at least a day or two had passed, and he would be dead indeed.

At last the needle touched zero; Dick felt his breath becoming faster, felt the air inside his helmet lose the clean bite of oxygen. He delayed as long as he could, then switched tanks. He could not resist gasping great lungfuls as the fresh, sweet air swept into his suit. Now all he could do was hope. Now was the critical time; now they might well expect him dead. If they came for him — he could think no more, hope no more. He was beyond thought and hope. He lay supine, his energy and will almost sapped, as close to death as he might be and yet live.

Overhead a square of light appeared; inquiring heads looked down. Dick lay rigid. Light played over his face. A tremor shook the concrete floor; one of the pirates jumped down from above.

A hand seized him, a rope was passed under his arms. Hanging limply, he was hauled up, out through the square of light, dropped roughly to the passage floor, and the noose was pulled free.

Dick opened his eye a slit; the pirate on top was now passing the line down to his comrade still in the cell. His back was to Dick. He rose to his feet, ran forward, pushed. The pirate threw back his head in astonishment, flung out his arms, sprawled headlong into the cell. Dick slid the hatch tight, bolted it home, then turned and ran down the passage.

Back to the surface, back to the surface! He ran as if a devil from hell were at his back — as indeed he was. Was he not fleeing the Basilisk?

With pounding heart and bulging eyes he sped along the passages, not knowing where he ran, eager only to run, to flee, to put the accursed place behind him.

He stopped to catch his breath. Three openings gaped in front of him; he set off along the middle passage; before long it slanted downward. He continued, not daring to turn back. Presently he came to another fork. It turned to the left, seemed to veer up, and this he chose. After a hundred feet it plunged for the bowels of the moon, and Dick, fearing pursuit, followed it down, willy-nilly.

Down, ever down, would it never turn up? Little side passages showed at intervals. Dick passed them by without a thought. When would the passage turn up?

A hundred yards later it leveled off, and Dick sighed with relief. A moment later he came to another fork, and this time he chose the tunnel to the right. Again the tunnel dived for the depths. Dick continued with a new fear nagging at his brain. Had he jumped from the frying pan into the fire? It was clear now that he was lost — lost in the lunar caves. Sam's chart was useless; probably these were passages Sam had never trod.

Down, down, down. Did any passages lead up? Dick halted, looked behind. The Basilisk was behind him. Better to die a clean death, better to die alone than at the will of the Basilisk.

The passage once more leveled, widened. Dick gazed with astonishment. The passage was paved, set with bits of rock arranged in strange looping patterns.

The feeling of age, of thousands, millions of years oppressed Dick's mind. Old beyond thought was this mosaic, old as the youth of the ancient moon; certainly no human hand had laid these colored bits of stone. Dick's breath came lighter; he moved on cautious, slow feet. Where the Basilisk came from there might be others; Dick had no wish to confront a score of the weird glow-eyed shapes in black hats and capes.

A flight of broad stairs opened before him, the treads hollowed and polished by a thousand centuries of use, but which aeon had seen the passing of these thousand centuries? In the airless chill, stone might stay unchanged from the beginning to the end of time.

The staircase widened to monumental proportions: fifty yards across, a hundred yards; they spread out past the glow of Dick's dome light. He stopped short, looking up the sweep of steps. The shadows on the steps made geometric patterns, bars of light and shade. And down ahead Dick glimpsed different shapes — complicated, delicate.

Slowly he moved down the steps; he was in an enormous cavern. And this cavern held a white city of intricate marble, fluted columns, spiral-peaked domes like unicorn horns, tall windows shaped like arrows — a strange fairyland city fading away through complicated shadows into indistinctness and darkness.

Dick stared transfixed. He took a step forward; there was furtive movement among the cold marble aisles and alleys: shapes watching him? Or shadows given life by his motion? Dick took another step, winced, blinked. The city seemed to be fading from his sight — drawing away, folding in on itself. Magic, a fairy city indeed? No. He laughed shakily. The power in his dome light was failing. The element flickered, went orange, red, faded. Blackness washed around Dick, and with it came that most elemental of fears: the fear of the dark.

# CHAPTER XVIII

## *The Eyes of the Basilisk (II)*

FOR WHATEVER INSTINCT had prompted him to bring spare oxygen and power, Dick gave thanks. Gratitude filled him to overflowing, brought tears to his eyes. Trembling, sobbing, his skin alternately chilled and hot, he slipped the new battery into place. Light burned again clear and strong against the wrought marble and curious façades of the lunar city.

Dick advanced step by step down the stairs, stepped off into one of the main avenues. Timorously he scanned the dark windows; nothing stirred, no white face appeared. He saw now that he trod the dust of ages. Wherever the Basilisk and creatures like him existed, it was not here in this ancient city. And yet — someone had trod this street before him; in the dust Dick discerned the tracks of space boots: Crazy Sam Baxter's?

Somewhat reassured, Dick walked down the central avenue. Pallid marble fronts, tall dark windows, façades embellished with ornate and complicated arabesques passed behind him. Beyond these fronts must lie curious treasures, coffers, bones, articles without Earthly name: a fascinating place to explore; sometime he'd come back, he promised himself, if only he were able to win to the surface.

He halted, looked behind. The stairs at the end of the terrace rose, but led toward the Security Station and the pirates; this route Dick did not dare take. But it was reasonable to assume that another similar stairway must lead up at the opposite end of the avenue.

He turned, ran ahead, giving no further heed to the antique build-ings. Sure enough, where the avenue ended, a stairs fully as broad as the ones on which he had descended, rose up into darkness. Dick bounded up, twenty feet at a jump. The staircase narrowed, bleak rock walls closed in. The steps came to an end; the passage slanted steeply up for a hundred yards, then leveled and broke into three. He hesitated. One of these must lead to the surface. Which one? He started tentatively down the passage to the right; it dipped sharply. He turned, came back to the junction, tried the passage to the left. After a hundred feet he met a blank wall. There was only the center way.

Dick proceeded with a curious sense of rightness; perhaps the same sixth sense which guides cats and dogs across thousands of miles to their homes. He broke out into an even wider passage, and it seemed to him there was a subtle familiarity to this new tunnel. Suddenly, he felt it must be the same passage into which he had first entered, the passage which opened near Crazy Sam's hut.

He hurried forward, running in great leaps, and the rock walls slid swiftly past him. A side passage opened to his right, a few yards later a passage opened to his left. He ignored both. Two minutes later he broke out upon the surface, with the great black sky above him and the sun blazing with the glistening furious incandescence which is seen only in the vacuum of space.

Dick heaved a grateful, tremulous sigh. Desolate, airless, sterile, the face of the moon at this instant looked as cheerful and welcome as his own white home among the Venusian flowers. But there was no time to waste; he ran to the shadow where he had left the rocket-raft. There it sat, undisturbed; in an instant he was aboard; in another he was sliding on streaming blue jets toward the observatory.

As he flew he considered what he must do on his return. It was a complicated situation. Certainly his father must be aroused; the news was too important to keep. If this were impossible, then he must confide in Professor Dexter; someone must authorize a message to the UN Bureau of Investigation and the Space Navy. And this idea posed a new problem: radio messages relayed to the Security Station transmitter would be intercepted by the Basilisk. He would naturally not allow this message to be broadcast; further, he might launch a punitive raid against the observatory. Dick crouched a little lower over the controls. Somehow a message must reach Earth; how, he did not know.

As soon as he reported what he knew, the matter would be out of his hands; his father or Professor Dexter was better able to cope with the problem than he was. What a wonderful relief to relax — and yet as soon as he reached the observatory, the Basilisk's spy would observe his arrival; the Basilisk would duly learn that Dick had returned and that his plans to raid Perseverine on Mars were known. Dick sighed. The problem was much too complex. He was tired; he wanted to sleep; he wanted to be relieved of responsibility.

The observatory grew large below him. Dick landed in the square and then ran toward the air lock. He passed within, slipped out of his space-suit, hurried to the lounge, which was empty.

Dick ran upstairs, his feet echoing hollowly on the steps. Where was everybody? The administration building seemed deserted. He hurried to the infirmary. The bed was empty; his father was gone.

He ran up to the room they shared — empty. Where was his father? Dick ran downstairs, through the tube to the mess hall. From the kitchen came the sound of activity. He looked in; Doc Mole stared.

"Where have you been?"

Dick said evasively, "Exploring...Where is everybody?"

Doc Mole rattled some pans, glaring at Dick from the corner of his eyes. "They're all out looking for you. You've put the camp in an uproar, my boy. When a man goes out and is gone more than six hours, people begin to think he's in trouble. Your poor father was at his wit's end — couldn't hold him in his sickbed. If I had my way they wouldn't allow kids the use of them rocket-rafts, especially when they prove to be irresponsible."

Dick turned slowly away and went back to the administration building. He threw himself into a chair, sat with his nerves taut as harp strings. Would it be better if he hid in his room revealing himself only to his father? Then the Basilisk spy would remain in ignorance; no, the idea was impractical. Crazy Sam's raft sat out in plain sight, and no power on Earth or moon could restrain the tongue of Doc Mole.

He rose to his feet; he could not bear to sit still. He must do something. He remembered his camera and the picture he had snapped of the Basilisk. He could develop it and have it ready to show his father.

He sprang to his feet, physically tired but keyed to galvanic tension.

From his space-suit pouch he took his camera, then ran up to Professor Dexter's darkroom.

He switched on the dim red glow, shut the door, pulled the exposed film from the camera. A few moments later, color and form appeared on the film. Dick rinsed it, clamped it into the enlarger. He focused with utmost care, then arranged and exposed the positive sheet.

The print was perfect. The Basilisk stood gaunt on the platform, looking balefully over the crowd of his myrmidons; and looking into the bulging golden eyes, Dick felt more than a stir of the terror which had held him riveted in place, helpless.

He turned up the lights, stood looking down at the picture. His composure returned to him; he felt half ashamed for yielding so completely to his emotions. The Basilisk was by no means supernatural; he had no real power to charm with his eyes. The spell which had held Dick to the window was the result of his own imagination — autosuggestion.

Dick bent more closely over the picture. Strange that the Basilisk, a denizen of the moon, should choose a garb which, while dramatic, was essentially Earthly; strange that nothing showed but his face. Dick pored over the photograph closely, then slid the print under a low-power microscope. The Basilisk's face was as if Dick stood two feet away. Dick stood rigid, almost forgetting to breathe, feeling as if he were on the verge of a momentous discovery.

Something was wrong. Along the cheekbone, down the neck, ran a peculiar line, and the flesh behind was a different texture than the dead frontal surface. The ears were even stranger, in that they were identical to those of a typical Earthman. The features of the Basilisk consisted, reasonably enough, of non-human eyes and facial structure; why then should they include ears which, in all their intricate convolutions, were unmistakably human?

Dick gave his attention to one of the eyes: first the great yellow disk, then the black central spot — he stopped short. The central spot was a human eye, set back a quarter-inch from the golden-yellow disk. The Basilisk was a hoax. The horrific face was a mask, clever beyond the imagination of most men — a mask compelling enough to cow five hundred depraved brutes, reduce Crazy Sam Baxter to doddering credulity, hypnotize Dick with fright.

He gave a disgusted bark of a laugh. What a fool he had made of himself! Once more he bent over the microscope, studied the brilliant black eye behind the golden masquerade.

Footsteps sounded outside; Dick raised his head. A hand took hold of the doorknob; the door opened. Outlined was the short, spare form of Professor Dexter. At the sight of Dick he stood stock-still, as if startled speechless. After a moment he found his voice, speaking as if the words choked in his throat, "When did you get back?"

Dick stared into the brilliant black eyes. The voice aroused a chord of memory...The gleaming eyes, the voice... Put a black broad-brimmed hat on Dexter, drape a black cape over the shoulders, translate the arrogance and hauteur into an insane hate for the human race. An icy wash rose up in Dick's body. He knew for certain the identity of the Basilisk.

# Chapter XIX

## The Great Martian Raid

IF PROFESSOR DEXTER felt Dick's recognition, he gave no sign of the knowledge. He stepped into the darkroom, carefully shut the door.

"When did you get back?" he repeated.

Dick knew that survival depended on his ability to dissemble during the next few moments. "I've been here about an hour." He was aware of the shake in his voice; perhaps Professor Dexter had not noticed.

"Where have you been all this time?" Professor Dexter asked casually — too casually.

Dick's mind worked like lightning, weighing a hundred subtleties. He could pretend not to trust Professor Dexter and lie; he could simulate complete confidence and report his adventures, of which Professor Dexter, as the Basilisk, was perfectly aware. In the end it probably would make no particle of difference. Dexter could not under any circumstances permit his double part to be revealed — at least not while in the guise of Professor Frederick Dexter and alone at the observatory without the support of his men.

So Dick hesitated, and to no avail. Professor Dexter took the initiative out of his hands. Advancing across the room, he picked up the photograph. "My word, what's this?" His voice was sharp, almost anxious.

"I snapped it at the Security Station," Dick blurted. "It's the Basilisk."

Dexter turned the brilliant black eyes full on Dick. "How clever you are, Dick! How enterprising and daring!" He noticed the sink full of rinsing water. "Brought it here and developed it, I see."

Dick had no reply to make. Dexter nodded. "Well, well." He reached up on a shelf, brought down a canister of white powder, shook a quantity into the water. "Sodium cyanide," he said absently. "I have a little work of my own to do." He replaced the canister, took down a brown glass bottle. The label read *Hydrochloric Acid.* "Perhaps you'd like to help me?" asked Dexter.

Dick watched, fascinated, as Professor Dexter unscrewed the bottle top. Dexter continued. "You're about to observe a rather interesting phenomenon. When I pour the acid into the tank, a gas will rise. The gas is sometimes called prussic acid, sometimes hydrogen cyanide. It has a pleasant odor — like almonds, I believe."

"I don't think —" Dick began.

Professor Dexter looked sidewise again, and Dick saw he was smiling. All pretense was now abandoned. "You don't think you care to participate? Perhaps not. But you should have considered all this before you went sneaking to places that were none of your business." He said as a casual afterthought, "The phenomenon I spoke of is called 'death'."

"But why," cried Dick. *"Why?"*

"Why must you die? Because at the moment you're the horseshoe nail in the story, for the want of which a kingdom was lost. Completely insignificant in yourself, you could cause me appreciable inconvenience. In two hours my ships, formerly the *African Star*, the *American Star*, the *Capella* and the *Canopus*, now completely reconditioned and fitted out as battleships, leave for Mars. No power on Earth or Moon can stop them. I plan to stay here; this observatory is my eye on the universe. At the telescope I watch ships come and go; I decide which shall live and which shall die."

"Ah," exclaimed Dick, "so that is why you killed Dr. Vrosnek and tried —"

Dexter nodded. "I executed Vrosnek and expected to become Chief Astronomer. But the trustees —" here Dexter's face burnt white as wax "— brought your father here instead. I resolved that he must die likewise; it was necessary that I work without interference. But you," Dexter looked at Dick with an expression almost of respect, "you have given me much more trouble than your father." His hand moved to the bottle of acid.

In an effort to stall for time, Dick asked, "Crazy Sam Baxter — how did you deceive him?"

Dexter laughed. "Crazy Sam was highly suggestible, just as you were. I hypnotized him, suggested to him that my men were lunar natives; Crazy Sam never knew differently. And now, Dick —"

Dick prepared to lunge forward, to fight for his life. Professor Dexter said, "I wouldn't if I were you, Dick. Because if you move, I'll throw the acid into your face instead of the tank."

Dick relaxed, stood hopelessly. Behind Dexter the doorknob turned. Dexter heard the click, backed warily to the side of the room. The door swung open, revealing the spare form of Sende.

"Ah, Sende," said Dexter cordially. "Come in. We were just speaking of you."

Sende's hawk-eyes moved from Dick to Dexter. "What's going on in here?" he asked in a voice like a file on sheet iron. He took a step forward.

Dexter moved with miraculous swiftness. He poured the acid in the tank. Dick yelled, "Look out, he's the Basilisk!" Dexter seized Sende, swung him into the darkroom, rushed out. The door slammed, the bolt clicked. From the developing tank came clouds of gas. Dick smelled bitter almonds.

Sende said something under his breath, then flung himself at the door.

"Don't breathe," cried Dick. "The air's full of prussic acid!" He pulled the stopper in the bottom of the tank; the mixture started to swirl down the drain, still fuming off the deadly gas.

Sende gave the door a tremendous kick; the lock gave, the door swung open. Choking and coughing, they pushed out into the clean air.

"Cursed creature!" cried Sende. "Where has he gone?"

He bounded off down the stairs; Dick, already starting to feel the effects of the prussic acid, followed more slowly. He reached the lounge in time to see Professor Dexter, clad in his space-suit, run from the administration building to Crazy Sam's rocket-raft, which was the only vehicle left at the observatory other than the dispatch boat. He jumped aboard and in a moment was soaring up over the crater wall.

Sende came back from the ward room, muttering under his breath. At the sight of Dick he stopped short. "What do you know about the Basilisk?"

Dick's stomach was palpitating; he felt nauseated, weak. Stumbling to one of the couches, he sat down, rubbed his head.

Sende came to look down at him. Dick said, "I think I'd better wait till my father comes back."

"He may be hours yet. He won't return till he gives up hope of finding you or his oxygen runs out."

With a trace of defiance Dick said, "I don't see why I should trust you. For all I know you're working with the Basilisk. After all, you trailed me out toward —"

Sende laughed. "I trailed you to see what you were up to, and you played a neat trick on me. As far as my working with the Basilisk —" He tossed a little plastic card on Dick's lap. It bore Sende's picture, the UN seal, and the words, "This will identify Arnold Barr Sende, Agent Extraordinary of the United Nations Bureau of Investigation. Bearer is hereby authorized to commandeer private property, regulate public and private transportation, direct local law officers."

Dick looked up in bewilderment. "Why — why didn't you tell me this before?"

Sende grinned his knife-slit grin. "I'm accustomed to working by myself. Admittedly I haven't learned very much. Suppose you tell me what I've missed."

Dick plunged into the tale of his adventures at the Security Station. When he had finished, Sende shook his head. "There's no use trying to send out a radio call. Dexter — the Basilisk — will already have cut us off. We'll take the dispatch boat and start off for Earth."

Remembering his experience on Sam's rocket-raft, Dick asked doubtfully, "Does the boat carry enough fuel for the trip?"

Sende nodded. "We'll load aboard extra oxygen and hydrogen. But come, we've got to hurry. You'd better leave a note for your father, then come out and help me fuel up."

Dick rose to his feet; fatigue and the effects of the gas made his legs wobbly. "Hurry now," said Sende. "You can sleep on the boat."

"But what shall I tell my father?"

"Tell him that you've gone to give information to the head office of the Bureau of Investigation, and that you'll be back in two or three days. Now hurry, every second counts."

Dick scribbled the message then, climbing into his space-suit, joined Sende, where he filled extra cylinders with liquid oxygen and hydrogen and strapped them to the side of the dispatch boat.

"There, that should be enough," said Sende. "Leaving the moon for Earth is easy enough; leaving Earth is seven times harder. Hurry now, jump in."

The dispatch boat nosed up on the full blast of the jets. Dick looked out over the desolate black and white moonscape, despondently wishing that there had been time for him to see his father. He glanced uneasily at Sende's spare back, remembering the distrust which he had felt ever since he had first known the man. He remembered the death of Kirdy, the mate aboard the *African Star*. How had Sende figured in this episode?

The ghostly ruins of the old Security Station came into view far below. Dick studied them with morbid fascination, recalling his experiences under that hard-seeming crust.

Sende turned his head, pointed. "Look."

Dick followed his finger toward one of the far concrete platforms. Four glinting metal shapes, minute across the distance, drifted majestically up into space.

"The *African Star*, the *American Star*, the *Capella* and the *Canopus*," said Sende. "Now the Basilisk's warships."

Together they watched the four ships swing away from the moon in a mighty arc, and one by one, line out toward the sultry gleam of Mars, gaining speed, plunging faster and faster, finally disappearing among the stars.

"They'll go on heavy acceleration," said Sende. "They'll reach Mars in three or four days."

"Can't we do anything?"

"Nothing I know of."

"But the Space Navy —"

Sende made a scornful sound. "The two corvettes? Like rabbits attacking wolves."

"To think that all this time," Dick said in an awed voice, "we've lived with the Basilisk, eaten at the same table —"

Sende turned him a bright, calculating glance. "That's the way it is with most people you know. What they seem and what they are make two different pictures. You'd better stretch out, catch some sleep. You'll be doing a lot of talking when we reach Earth."

# CHAPTER XX

## *Attack!*

DICK AWOKE WITH A START to find Sende bent over the dispatch boat's little ship-to-ship radio. "What's the matter?" asked Dick anxiously. Sende signaled him to be quiet, continued to listen. A tinny little voice came from the speaker, words Dick could not distinguish. He raised himself from the couch, came closer to the radio.

"—now we see you...Good...Your course is almost opposite ours. Turn end for end, brake with full power. We'll do the rest."

"Right," said Sende into the microphone. He sprang to the controls. The constellations swung past the window in a giddy rush.

Dick clutched the seat. "Who was that?"

"The Space Navy," said Sende, accenting the words wryly. "They picked us up on their radar."

Dick said eagerly, "But that's lucky — they can radio to Earth, and the Earth station can warn Perseverine..."

Sende nodded. "There's always that possibility."

Dick gave him a puzzled glance, but Sende had no more to say.

Ten minutes passed, then Dick spied the escort corvettes crossing the sky a few miles to the left. "There they are."

Sende nodded, adjusted the controls; the gap between them narrowed. Sende bent once more over the radio.

"Are you sending over a boat for us?"

The answer came back. "No. Get into your space-suits and jump across."

"What about the dispatch boat?"

"I'll send a man to take it back to the observatory. Wait till we approach to a hundred feet."

"Good." Sende turned to Dick. "Looks like we jump out into nothing."

Dick stepped into his space-suit. "I hope we don't miss. I've had all of drifting through space that I want."

Sende laughed grimly, zipped together the seam on his suit, clamped down the dome. "Ready?" The words now came through the radio inside Dick's helmet.

"Ready," said Dick.

They entered the air lock, closed the inner, opened the outer door, and stood poised, waiting.

One of the corvettes edged closer. "Now," said Sende, "I'll go first." Without further words he launched himself.

Dick watched the long figure move away, gliding easily through the vacuum. Then he poised, tensed his muscles, jumped. The corvette expanded; the silhouette blacked out the stars; the door to the air lock grew larger. His jump had been nearly perfect, he missed the open air lock by only two feet. Sende reached out a hand, pulled him in. Behind Sende was a third figure, the man who would pilot the dispatch boat back to the moon.

Three minutes later, out of his space-suit, Dick found himself face to face with Commander Franchetti.

"Now suppose you tell me what's happened," Franchetti said to Sende.

Sende indicated Dick. "There's the lad who knows the whole story."

Franchetti turned to Dick. "Well?"

Dick drew a deep breath. "There's a lot to tell. It boils down to the fact that the Basilisk is using the old Security Station for a base; and that he told me, when he thought I'd never live to tell about it, that he was on his way to raid Perseverine, on Mars."

Sende said, "I saw four ships — the *African Star*, the *American Star*, the *Capella* and the *Canopus* — leave the Security Station and line out for Mars. There's no question in my mind but that Dick's information is correct. I think you'd better radio Earth—" he handed Franchetti his credentials. Franchetti glanced at them, returned them "— and ask them to notify Perseverine to prepare for the raid, or possibly evacuate the city completely."

Franchetti nodded. "I'll take care of it at once." He stepped around the glass panel which separated the radio cage from the saloon. Dick and Sende saw him giving terse instructions to the radio operator. The operator turned dials, flipped switches; Franchetti bent over the microphone, spoke at some length, listened, spoke again. Finally he straightened up, returned to the saloon.

"They're calling Perseverine now. As soon as they get an answer they'll call us back." He looked at Dick. "How did you happen to hear all this about the Basilisk?"

Dick told his story again. Commander Franchetti shook his head, whistled. "I always figured old Dexter for one of these ivory-tower lads, pure scientist, not a nerve or an emotion in his body. Perhaps a little sour, but never in a million years would I have picked him for a pirate." He rubbed his chin. "Now that I think of it, Dexter seemed to know a great deal of the history and philosophy of piracy. Not that the knowledge was suspicious in itself, but it goes to show what he had on his mind."

The radio operator tapped on the glass. Franchetti jumped up. "That'll be Navy headquarters."

Dick and Sende followed him around into the radio operator's cubicle. Franchetti bent to the microphone. "Franchetti on the *Theseus* speaking."

A few seconds passed while the radio waves traversed space. Then came the reply. "This is Commodore Hallmeier. We can't get through to Perseverine. The station is dead."

Sende muttered softly, "I thought as much. One of Dexter's men sabotaged the transmitter."

Franchetti leaned close to the microphone. "What are my orders, sir?"

The crisp voice said, "We will continue trying to raise Mars, although I suspect without success. You will proceed with all possible speed to Mars, seek out the pirate ships, attack them."

Franchetti stammered, "Very good, sir."

He straightened, turned slowly to Sende and Dick. "Attack, says the

Commodore." He shook his head ruefully. "Attack four ships with the two corvettes." He turned to the radio operator. "Notify Eden in the *Achilles*, Rogers...Two gravities toward Mars." He looked back at Dick and Sende. "I'll find you quarters after we get under way; until then you'd better make yourselves comfortable here in the saloon."

A moment later the *Theseus* swerved around, nosed up toward Mars; the weight of two gravities gripped all aboard.

Dick sat by the port, watching the scarred black and white globe of the moon receding. By now his father would have returned to the observatory and found his note, and so would be correspondingly relieved of anxiety. Dick laughed sourly. Little did he realize the true situation.

Sende turned his hawk's profile toward Dick. "You don't seem to like space travel, Dick."

"No. I'm tired of it. I'd rather be safe back at the observatory, although I've had nothing there but excitement since I landed."

"Even before, as I recall."

Dick nodded. "There's something that's been puzzling me. What happened to Kirdy, the mate with the mustache?"

Sende shrugged. "We had something of a disagreement. He wanted to send radio messages to the Basilisk, and I — since that is what I had come aboard the *African Star* specifically to prevent — decided that he shouldn't. We had a tussle and poor Kirdy wound up with a broken neck. I decided that he would arouse the least attention under the hatch to the bridge, so I dropped him there. Any more questions?"

"I can't think of any right now."

Commander Franchetti came into the saloon, sat down heavily. "You chaps got your wills made out? Because if you haven't, you'd better get busy. These corvettes make good little scout ships, but as far as attacking even one of the Basilisk's ships —" He shook his head despondently. "We're underarmed; nothing but three little popguns to each ship. The Basilisk's ships have cannon and rocket launchers enough to blow up a mountain. We're undermanned; the man I had sent to fly the boat back to the observatory leaves us short a gunner."

"I used to be a pretty good hand on the target range," said Sende. "You could put me to work."

Dick said, "I'd like a shot at the Basilisk myself."

Commander Franchetti nodded. "Good. I'll put both of you to use. But right now I'll show you where you'll be sleeping, and you can turn in if you care to. It's nothing fancy — just a couple of pipe-berths. We're not a luxury passenger ship."

"Anything," said Dick with a sigh. "I'm so tired I could sleep standing up."

When Dick awoke, Earth and Moon were far astern; they were passing through the Graveyard, now safe as a country meadow, with the Basilisk's entire fleet on its way to Mars.

Dick and Sende became assistants to port and starboard gunners respectively, and gun drill did much to relieve the strain on Dick's nerves. The atmosphere of the ship was one of gloom and foreboding; Cobbett, the gunner whose assistant Dick had become, was openly bitter. "What's the use of sending us in toy spaceboats all the way out to Mars to get killed? They could do us in just as proper by asking us to jump out of the air lock forty miles above Earth, and it would save a lot of time."

"Well," Dick ventured, "maybe we could —" he paused.

"Could what?" asked Cobbett sarcastically. "Paint horrible faces on the bow and scare 'em to death? Hah! That's about the size of it. If you ask me this is another blasted Navy snafu, and me, Winston Churchill Cobbett, being stuck for the check."

"But would they send us out if there wasn't a good reason?"

Cobbett laughed. "Dick, my boy, when you've been in the Navy as long as I have, you'll know that anything is possible. Now enough of this gab; pay a little attention to the gun."

"You've been doing all the talking," snapped Dick.

"Well, maybe I have," Cobbett admitted. "But I expect to be cashing in my chips in two or three days, and I've got lots of talking I want to get done before then. But while I'm talking, you're supposed to be learning how to handle this peashooter here, so that after I get mine, you can step up like a gentleman and take what the Basilisk's got ordered for you."

Dick grinned. "The Basilisk has tried to get me a few times already, and I'm still here. Maybe he'll miss again."

"Maybe, maybe not. But no more of your lip now. Out there's Sirius. Let me see you load, sight and fire in eight seconds, Navy regulation — only don't pull the trigger. We might need that very same shell for a chap who calls himself the Basilisk."

"Why do we use these old-fashioned guns?" asked Dick. "I should think radar-guided missiles would be more effective."

"Certainly they'd be more effective," snorted Cobbett. "There just aren't any. We haven't made weapons since the Security Station was abandoned. The Space Navy, after all, is only a few months old. So we use these antiques." He slapped the gun barrel contemptuously.

"Well, at least if we don't have them, the Basilisk doesn't either."

"That's cold comfort," grumbled Cobbett. "What difference does it make what kind of rocket blows you to perdition? It's the blowing-up itself that's important. You can take it from me," and he tapped Dick's chest, "take it from me, W. C. Cobbett, that whoever comes out of this fracas alive can count himself lucky."

Dick forced a laugh. "You're a pessimist."

"Pessimist? Me?" Cobbett seemed genuinely astonished. "I'm no pessimist. I'm not even a realist. I joined the Space Navy to see the universe, like the recruiting poster says. I'm an optimist. I'm always looking for the best side of things. I just don't see any best side. Do you know what Commodore Hallmeier has written beside all our names?"

"No," said Dick in a subdued voice, "I've no idea."

"Well, I'll tell you. It's just one word: 'Expendable'."

# CHAPTER XXI

## *Battle*

MARS SHONE AHEAD like a fire opal, the desert reds and russets, the gray-greens and blue of the polar frost-caps shimmering to the windy movement of the atmosphere. Commander Franchetti sat crouched at the radar controls, sweeping space ahead. "We can't be too far behind them," he muttered to Sende. "They had no reason to hurry; they still have no reason. Perseverine sits there like a ripe plum; there's nothing to stop them but the local police force." He stared gloomily into the screen. "We'll keep the Basilisk busy for ten minutes anyway. He'll know he's been in a fight."

Dick scanned the mottled disk of Mars. "Where is Perseverine?"

Franchetti pointed. "See there, that slanting line?"

Dick nodded.

"That's the Peripher Canal. See where it crosses that low range of mountains?"

"Yes."

"Well, that little dark spot between the canal and the mountains is Perseverine." He looked across space a long moment. "We should be picking up the Basilisk pretty soon."

"Unless he's already gone to work," Sende remarked coolly.

Franchetti shrugged, flipped a switch on the command-circuit. "All personnel into space-suits; stand by battle stations."

"Why space-suits?" Dick asked.

"So that if we take a hit, the loss of air won't kill us."

Dick made his way to the gear locker — the corvettes were decelerating on two gravities — climbed into his space-suit.

Time dragged past. Mars spread wide its dusty red plains. Returning to the bridge, Dick found Franchetti and Sende staring tensely into the radar screen. He heard Franchetti mutter, "Strange… Can't understand where they've gone to. Perseverine seems undisturbed…"

A sudden idea startled Dick into speech. "Unless we've passed them in space and they're coming up behind us!"

Franchetti turned him a surprised glance; Dick regretted his brashness. But Franchetti, after a moment's hesitation, said a little sheepishly, "It's a thought." He swung the control knob; the radar projector twisted to scan the sky astern. Instantly four blobs of orange light flashed on the screen. Franchetti barked into the intercom microphone, "Battle stations, double-quick; stand by for action… Enemy dead astern!"

Dick ran to his gun station, where he found Cobbett leisurely clamping down his helmet. "We only die once," said Cobbett. "This seems to be it."

Dick's heart and throat were too full for speech.

"Attach your safety belts!" Franchetti's voice came sharp through the earphones. "We're going to be pretty busy."

Dick had barely time to snap his elastic safety belt to the stanchion when the ship lurched sharply to the side. Mars rolled crazily past the port. Dick caught a flicker astern, sunlight reflecting on distant hulls. Cobbett bent over his gun.

The ship swung further, the hulls disappeared once more behind the stern; the horizons of Mars expanded tremendously. "Franchetti's going to hang close to the surface," said Cobbett, "where their radar-guided missiles, if they have any, won't be effective. Although," he added, "if they have automatic weapons and we're still stuck with these antiques, I'm resigning from the Navy — effective at once."

Dick said nervously, "Where could the Basilisk get automatic weapons? They haven't been made for years."

Cobbett shook his head sardonically. "I wouldn't put anything past him." He stared up at a great hulk looming suddenly down across the port quarter. From the black bow an orange spark flickered for an instant. "By golly," said Cobbett, in a hushed voice, "they're shooting at us. Missed, I guess. If they hadn't —"

Into the earphones came Franchetti's voice. "Gunners, fire at targets as soon as they come into range."

Cobbett growled between his teeth. "Out in space, range is as far as you can see. Well — here goes." He squinted through his range finder, turned dials, touched the trigger button. The gun lanced blue and yellow light, the corvette quivered with the recoil. A moment later a flame splashed across the pirate ship. "You hit them!" cried Dick. "You hit them!"

"Good shot, Cobbett," came Franchetti's voice.

Cobbett muttered, "They probably never felt it." He motioned impatiently to Dick, "Hurry up with the shells; this isn't a Sunday-school picnic."

The pirate ship seemed little affected by the hit; its guns sparked and winked. By dint of wild dodging Franchetti managed to draw safely away.

The surface of Mars came closer and closer; Dick glimpsed clouds of red dust blowing across the deserts. The corvette swooped up in a change of direction so violent that Dick's eyes went dim, skimmed close over the ground. Alongside and a little astern flew the *Achilles*. Cobbett lowered his head, peered into the sky. "Franchetti's trying to bring them low where he can outmaneuver them." He shook his head. "Unless the Basilisk just wants to drop down for a romp, he'll stay up and take pot shots whenever he gets our range."

"But what can we do?"

Cobbett shrugged. "Duck, dodge, fire a shot or two, take our punishment."

Dick pressed close to the port. "I can see two, three ships. They're just waiting. Now one of them is dropping down."

A dark shadow fell across the port. Cobbett aimed and fired again and again. Then the corvette shuddered, jarred, as if struck by a hammer. Air sucked past Dick.

"We're hit," said Cobbett matter-of-factly. "Come on now, let's have the shells; I want to get a few of those devils before I cash in."

The corvette was plunging toward the ground; it started to whirl and twist. Dick clung to the stanchion, sure that his last moment was upon him. But only a half-mile above the surface Franchetti steadied the ship, brought its nose up.

"She's hit in the rear tubes," muttered Cobbett. "Franchetti's balancing her as if he were walking a tightrope." He looked out the port. "Here comes the Basilisk. We can't get away. We can't maneuver, all we can do is fire our popguns."

Sweat poured down Dick's forehead into his eyes; outside he saw two of the pirate ships cruising deliberately, ominously, closer.

Cobbett peered into his range finder, adjusted his sights with the nicest precision, muttering under his breath all the time. He fired. The bridge on the nearest ship exploded; Cobbett yelled in exultation. "There's one done for! By golly, I'll die happy!"

The pirate ship drifted off to the side; settled grandly toward Mars. The other swung close, the gun ports blazed angry orange.

Dick felt blinding white light, staggered. Something pulled at his middle, nearly wrenched him in two. For a moment he was blind, numb. He thrashed out with his arms, pulled himself to his feet. The strain at his middle eased. Behind, a great irregular hole gaped in the hull; at his feet lay Cobbett, a spear-shaped fragment of metal protruding from his chest.

Dick limped to the gun. He threw a shell into the breech. There — a pirate ship, insolently close. Dick touched the trigger button, saw the shell explode against one of the gun ports.

The corvette was settling in a series of lurches and swoops, which made aim difficult. Dick noticed the other corvette, slightly below, falling like an autumn leaf. But only three pirate ships hung in the sky; Cobbett's shot had sent one down.

In a daze Dick loaded, aimed, fired — loaded, aimed, fired. He felt a thud from below — another hit. A miracle that the ship was still under any kind of control.

The pirate ships were in a line now, gun ports like a row of black teeth. Dick stared. What was that behind? He blinked. A silver cylinder came gliding down upon the battle, a ship half as large again as the largest pirate ship. It swept in parallel to the pirates; from a row of modest-looking tubes came puffs of white smoke. An instant later searing incandescence blotted away the sky.

Dick felt a pressure at his back; he blinked over his shoulder with dazzled eyes. Sende stood behind him. "What is that ship?" Dick croaked.

Sende grunted. "I suppose it's the new Navy cruiser; they seem to have rushed it to completion, got it in commission just in time."

Out in space the cruiser now faced only two ships. Again came the white puffs. Dick hid his eyes; the flash of light burned through his eyelids.

"Two gone," he heard Sende say. "I wonder which ship the Basilisk is on."

Dick looked below; the rusty sands of Mars were close under the hull. At a little distance lay the hulk of the ship Cobbett had shot down. From the lifeboat bay came a small gray craft, shaped like a needle; oversize jets projected from the stern.

Dick cried with sudden intuition, "There he goes now — there goes the Basilisk!" He staggered to the gun, twisted the dials, but Sende pushed him away. He swung the barrel, aiming by a sixth sense, touched the button. Time passed while a man could take a breath. Then the gray craft, darting across the desert, became a blotch of flame, a puff of dirty smoke. And from overhead a third and final flash blinded the sky.

# CHAPTER XXII

## *A Glimpse at the Future*

SHELTERED FROM THE EQUATORIAL WINDS by Mount Helion, watered by the Peripher Canal, Perseverine seemed to Dick completely beautiful and peaceful. Low houses, white, pale blue and green, were scattered among the black-green Martian feather trees, the gray-green banks and lawns of shaggy moss, the cucumber-green century plants which, imported from Earth, grew to an enormous size on Mars.

In the background rose ruddy Mount Helion; on the slopes lay the ruins of the ancient Martian city Kron — stone arches, colonnades, platforms, walls now crumbling, soft gray, mellow.

Dick's first act was to send a trans-space message to his father from the now-functioning Perseverine transmitter. Returning to the Hotel Grand-Laurent where the uninjured survivors of the battle had been billeted, Dick took a hot bath in a tub ten feet long and four feet wide. A blast of warm fragrant air dried him; returning to his bedroom, he found three complete new outfits laid out on the bed. He dressed himself in a soft blue suit and went along the arcade to the lobby, where he met Sende.

Sende looked Dick over from head to foot. "Looks like they're taking care of you pretty well."

"It's wonderful," said Dick. He looked doubtfully at his new clothes. "But I've no idea how I'm going to pay for it all."

Sende laughed. "At the point of a gun, you couldn't force anyone in Perseverine to take your money."

Dick looked uncomfortably around the lobby. "I don't care for all this... well, attention."

"You'd better get used to it. Newspapers all over the System are running the story of the Basilisk; you've come in for a lot of publicity."

Dick grimaced. "I was hoping that my mother wouldn't hear too much of what's been going on."

Sende laughed. "Not a chance. If you go back to Miracle Valley, you'll step right off the ship into Dick Murdock Week."

Dick shook his head decidedly. "Not if I can help it. I won't have anything to do with it."

"Sometimes there's not much you can do."

Commodore Hallmeier entered the lobby, waved his hand in a smart gesture that was almost a salute. "Well, Dick, I see you're in good shape again."

"Yes, sir," said Dick. Commodore Hallmeier, a large, spare man with icicle-gray eyes, had a presence which rather awed him.

"You've been of great help to us. I won't go into exact detail now, but I intend to see that you get the recognition you deserve."

"I've an idea that the newspapers have taken the matter out of your hands," remarked Sende.

The Commodore's eyes twinkled; he suddenly seemed less austere. "Yes, I imagine that they won't leave much unsaid. Still, there may be a few words I can put in here and there."

"Really sir," Dick burst out, "I wish you wouldn't."

The Commodore shook his head. "Modesty is one of the old-fashioned virtues — a little out of place, I'm afraid, in this present-day world. Well, that's neither here nor there." He studied Dick a moment. "I understand you're bent on a career in astronomy?"

Dick considered. "I've more or less taken it for granted," he said slowly, "but I'm not completely sure that it's how I want to spend my life."

"Like action and adventure too much, do you?"

"I suppose so. Not that astronomers don't have adventures, but I'm more interested in visiting stars than studying them through a telescope."

Commodore Hallmeier looked off through the arch, into the purple Martian distances. "And that's certainly our next step — out to the stars. We've still a hundred problems to solve, but as sure as man was never content with the boundaries of Earth, he will never be content with the boundaries of the Solar System."

"It shouldn't be too long now," said Sende.

"There'll be new cities, new empires, ships carrying cargoes we can't even imagine. And human beings constituted as they are, there'll be new pirates, new Basilisks. They'll have to be dealt with, and harshly. Our Space Navy is in its infancy, but we're expanding. Before the settlers and traders and miners go out to the far planets, the Navy will have been there first, exploring, experimenting, making contact with whatever other races happen to exist."

Dick's eyes glowed, he caught his breath to speak, but the Commodore went on.

"There'll be a hundred ships on patrol, a score of naval stations. We'll need men in the Space Navy — the best men we can find." He looked Dick full in the eyes. "Astronomers are very useful and important, but I think you could be of more use to the world and to yourself in the Space Navy."

Dick started to speak. The Commodore held up his hand. "Don't give me an answer now. You've still got a few years ahead of you. Go back to the observatory, talk it over with your father. Tell him that Commodore Hallmeier has offered you the commission of ensign in the Space Navy; that after you've finished the regulation course at the Las Vegas Space-Training Academy, he has a place for you on his personal staff. Talk it over, explore all the angles, then write me a letter."

Dick drew a deep breath. "Commodore, I'll do as you say, but I know what the answer will be right now. I want to accept your offer very much, and I know my father will agree."

Commodore Hallmeier smiled faintly. "Very well, Dick. You report to me on your seventeenth birthday and I'll have your appointment to the Academy waiting for you."

"Thank you very much," said Dick.

"Don't thank me," said Commodore Hallmeier. "I'll be proud to have you on my staff." He turned away. "In about two years then." He saluted casually and walked away across the lobby.

JACK VANCE was born in 1916 to a well-off California family that, as his childhood ended, fell upon hard times. As a young man he worked at a series of unsatisfying jobs before studying mining engineering, physics, journalism and English at the University of California Berkeley. Leaving school as America was going to war, he found a place as an ordinary seaman in the merchant marine. Later he worked as a rigger, surveyor, ceramicist, and carpenter before his steady production of sf, mystery novels, and short stories established him as a full-time writer.

His output over more than sixty years was prodigious and won him three Hugo Awards, a Nebula Award, a World Fantasy Award for lifetime achievement, as well as an Edgar from the Mystery Writers of America. The Science Fiction and Fantasy Writers of America named him a grandmaster and he was inducted into the Science Fiction Hall of Fame.

His works crossed genre boundaries, from dark fantasies (including the highly influential *Dying Earth* cycle of novels) to interstellar space operas, from heroic fantasy (the *Lyonesse* trilogy) to murder mysteries featuring a sheriff (the Joe Bain novels) in a rural California county. A Vance story often centered on a competent male protagonist thrust into a dangerous, evolving situation on a planet where adventure was his daily fare, or featured a young person setting out on a perilous odyssey over difficult terrain populated by entrenched, scheming enemies.

Late in his life, a world-spanning assemblage of Vance aficionados came together to return his works to their original form, restoring material cut by editors whose chief preoccupation was the page count of a pulp magazine. The result was the complete and authoritative *Vance Integral Edition* in 44 hardcover volumes. Spatterlight Press is now publishing the VIE texts as ebooks, and as print-on-demand paperbacks.

# Colophon

This book was printed using Adobe Arno Pro as the primary text font, with NeutraFace used on the cover.

This title was created from the digital archive of the Vance Integral Edition, a series of 44 books produced under the aegis of the author by a worldwide group of his readers. The VIE project gratefully acknowledges the editorial guidance of Norma Vance, as well as the cooperation of the Department of Special Collections at Boston University, whose John Holbrook Vance collection has been an important source of textual evidence.

Special thanks to R.C. Lacovara, Patrick Dusoulier, Koen Vyverman, Paul Rhoads, Chuck King, Gregory Hansen, Suan Yong, and Josh Geller for their invaluable assistance preparing final versions of the source files.

Source: Norma Vance; Digitize: Richard Chandler, Joel Hedlund; Diff: Kurt Harriman, Damien G. Jones; Tech Proof: Rob Friefeld; Text Integrity: Rob Friefeld, Kurt Harriman, Tim Stretton; Implement: Donna Adams, Derek W. Benson; Security: Paul Rhoads; Compose: Joel Anderson; Comp Review: Marcel van Genderen, Charles King, Paul Rhoads, Robin L. Rouch; Update Verify: Rob Friefeld, Robert Melson, Paul Rhoads; RTF-Diff: Charles King, Hans van der Veeke; Textport: Patrick Dusoulier, Suan Hsi Yong; Proofread: Mike Barrett, Carina Björklind, Carl Goldman, Charles King, Roderick MacBeath, Fernando Maldonado, David Reitsema, Ivo Steijn, Gabriel Stein, Cameron Thornley, Russ Wilcox

Artwork (maps based on original drawings by Jack and Norma Vance): Paul Rhoads, Christopher Wood

Book Composition and Typesetting: Joel Anderson

Art Direction and Cover Design: Howard Kistler

Proofing: Chuck King, Steve Sherman

Jacket Blurb: John Vance

Management: John Vance, Koen Vyverman

CPSIA information can be obtained
at www.ICGtesting.com
Printed in the USA
BVOW08s1041171217
503037BV00001B/137/P